INSIDE . . .

The door opened to a dimly lit room lined with tall bookcases. As soon as I stepped in, the door closed behind me. The marble tiles on the floor were arranged in alternating black and white like a chessboard and I had the unnerving feeling that I was a pawn, but I did my best to remain calm. It was quiet—too quiet, as if it had been soundproofed. A stuffed polar bear head with red glass eyes hung over the mantel.

My resolve to remain calm didn't last long. In less than two minutes I was up, peering anxiously out the window—barred from the outside. Suddenly I couldn't wait any longer. I strode to the door and twisted the knob. It wouldn't turn. Scarcely able to believe it, I twisted it again. I wrenched at it until my hand hurt. Then I bent to peer at the crack between the door and the doorjamb. The bolt was shot into place . . .

JANICE
HARRELL

FATAL MAGIC is an original publication of Avon Books. This work has never before appeared in book form. Any similarity to actual persons or events is purely coincidental.

AVON BOOKS
A division of
The Hearst Corporation
1350 Avenue of the Americas
New York, New York 10019

Published by arrangement with the author
Library of Congress Catalog Card Number: 93-91657
ISBN: 0-380-77327-9
RL: 5.6

First Avon Flare Printing: February 1994

AVON FLARE TRADEMARK REG. U.S. PAT. OFF. AND IN OTHER COUNTRIES, MARCA REGISTRADA, HECHO EN U.S.A.

Printed in the U.S.A.

RA 10 9 8 7 6 5 4 3 2 1

Chapter 1

It was a typical night at the parapsychology lab where I had a part-time job. I had a garden-variety nut on the phone and had propped the phone up on my shoulder so I could keep working while he talked.

"I can make volcanoes erupt," he said. "I caused Mount St. Helens'. That was one of my big ones. You people really ought to study me."

"Uh-huh," I said, neatly slipping a yellow flimsy into a file folder.

"I'm working on Mauna Loa now," said the caller.

"Right," I said. "Well, sir, if you'll just give me your name and address, I'll send you some information." I pulled a manila envelope and wrote his name and address on it.

"I think I could really help you guys," he said.

"Right. You should be getting the information within three days to a week. Good-bye." I stuffed the pamphlets and forms into the envelope, slapped on a stamp, and put it in the mail basket. Too bad they didn't have a basket labelled nut cases. It would be overflowing.

Dr. Burrows came out of the experiment room. "Blythe," he blinked. "I thought you'd already left."

"Not till nine." I smiled brightly. It was eight-thirty and I'd had such a steady stream of calls I hadn't able to start my homework. My job was to e regular secretary on the evening the lab te. It stayed open late Tuesdays to make people who were participating in experi-ts to come in after they finished work.

As far as I could make out, the kind of people Dr. Burrows wanted were not the ones who said they could cause volcanoes to erupt but the ones who could predict what was going to be on the face of a card before he flipped it over. It all sounded pretty boring to me. Our lab was only an outpost of the more important parapsychology lab at Duke, so I figured maybe the guys at Duke kept all the really good experiments for themselves.

"Well, go on home." Dr. Burrows waved me away. "If the phone rings, I can answer it."

I didn't wait for a second invitation. I stuffed my books in my book bag and sprinted for the door. Lately I dreaded the long drive home along the deserted highway, but part-time jobs were hard to come by in our area and I knew I was lucky to have one where I could usually do homework between phone calls.

Outside in the parking lot, the night seemed unusually dark. I couldn't see either the moon or the stars. Turning my key in the ignition, I listened to the motor cough, then began edging out of the parking lot. Suddenly my heart began pounding wildly and I realized my palms were sticky on the steering wheel. I had had outbursts of panic a lot ever since . . . But I had decided I wasn't going to think about that, I reminded myself, pushing the terrible memory away. I stopped the car a minute and tried to make myself breathe regularly. I was perfectly fine, I told myself. Soon I would be completely over it—if I could just forget what happened. Slowly I inched the car out onto the roadway.

My car had been made up from parts of three different cars and it didn't exactly have great pickup. It had quite a few little peculiarities, too, like I couldn't close the door on the right unless the door on the left was open. But the price had been right, which was the main thing. Money was tight at our house since my mother died a year and a half ago and Dad and I had been left with a lot of debts. We had moved into a smaller, cheaper place further out of town, where Dad said he could keep chickens and make extra money. He was always full of ideas like that. But the chickens got feather droop or something and the next thing I knew he had sold them and had come up with a new idea. He signed up for the naval reserve. As he explained it, he only had to go do one weekend a month and then two weeks in the summer and for that he got a very nice little pay supplement. Too bad that all of a sudden there was a big blowup in the Middle East and Dad's reserve unit was called up. I wasn't even that surprised. It was always that way with Dad's plans. Now, instead of making extra money, we were going to be living on even less. "You'll have to go stay with Grandma," Dad said as soon as he got the notification that his latest plan had gone splat all over my life.

"In Oregon? You must be kidding," I wailed. "I'm staying right here."

"You can't stay here by yourself!"

"I don't see why not. I can drive a car. I can write checks. I'm practically grown. I can take care of myself."

Dad clutched me close to him. "We're just unlucky, pet. Everything happens to us."

"Don't be silly," I said. "I'll bet you won't be gone long. I'll be perfectly fine."

Dad and I weren't a bit alike. I was more like my mother—levelheaded. I had Mom's looks, too—long legs, dark hair, and steady brown eyes.

I had felt more grown-up than my father for years, but I knew I had to prove to him that I was completely in control or he would make me go to Oregon to stay with Grandmother after all. Unfortunately, driving home now from the lab, I wasn't feeling at all in control. I steered the car carefully around the curve that skirted the abandoned quarry, and my headlights glanced off the dull metal of the low guardrail. Even though it was too dark for me to see the quarry below, I hated knowing it sat there filled with cold, stagnant water. My car's motor rumbled uncertainly. The road straightened and I stared ahead, hoping I wasn't in for car trouble. "I'll be fine," I muttered to myself. Just as I was persuading myself of that, my headlights flickered. I would have to have the car checked, I thought. There must be a short in the electrical system. The hyphenated yellow center line of the road sped past on my left and my headlights reached tentatively into the road ahead. Then all at once my lights went off. It was so dark I might have been driving off a cliff for all I knew. I hit the brakes and glanced around me frantically. I was miles now from the parapsychology center, yet probably still a good two miles from home. At first I couldn't think straight. But once my eyes got used to the darkness, I realized I could still make out the white lines along the side of the road. The overcast skies were letting through a glimmer of light, enough to make out the white line, though not much else. Gritting my teeth, I held onto the steering wheel with whitened knuckles and fixed my eyes on that white side line. I had to get home—that was my one thought. I started up the car because I didn't know what else to do.

My eyes were practically bugging out of my skull from staring at the white line, when suddenly, too late, I saw a single beam bearing down on me from ahead. My breath sucked in as I slammed on my brakes and swerved sharply to miss it. The motorcycle went narrowly past me with a loud roar, then my car skidded and turned sideways in the road. I sat in my car trembling. My car must have crept over the center line without my realizing it. And, of course, the motorcycle driver hadn't seen me because I had no lights.

I took a few shuddering breaths, then turned my car back into the right lane. Somehow after that I doggedly managed to keep going toward town, but I hardly knew what I was doing. A dull roaring sounded in my ears, but I was so freaked out that I just assumed it was some kind of aftereffect of shock. Then I noticed the light in my rearview window. A single headlight, a star of brightness, shone in my rearview mirror. The motorcycle was following me. Frightened now, I speeded up, but he went faster, too, keeping the same steady distance behind me. Fatalism crept into my heart like cold water. He wanted to kill me. I was going to die. But somehow I kept my foot on the gas.

At last I saw the glow of streetlights ahead and my heart gave a thump of relief. A minute later I was coming up to a red light. Around me were fire hydrants, street signs—all the signs of life and habitation that meant safety. Everything suddenly seemed so normal that without thinking I slowed for the stop light, but then I glanced over my shoulder and saw the biker, a dark shape waiting about a block behind me. I jabbed my foot on the gas and ran right through the red light. The next light was yellow. I didn't even slow down for it. My tires squealed as I turned onto Hammond Road. I was afraid to look in the rearview window. All I could think about was home. Hammond Road ran through farmlands, but on one side was a line of small houses that had been built close together. Light bled through their curtained windows, but they looked deserted. After a couple of miles, the houses gave out and dark woods loomed up on my left. I was almost home. We had moved to a small new subdivision out past the edge of town.

Maybe I should have gone somewhere else so the biker wouldn't know where I lived, but that never occurred to me. Like a horse that runs back into a burning barn, I had the wrongheaded feeling that home was safe. I saw our subdivision's sign, Holmhaven, and turned in so sharply that my left wheel ran over the edge of the chrysanthemum bed beside the sign. Then with a sudden wrench of the steering wheel I turned into my own driveway. No sooner had the car rolled to a stop than I flung open my door and ran to the house. My hands trembled as I fit my house key into the lock. I darted into the house, snapped the dead bolt shut behind me, and leaned against the door sick with relief.

"Blythe? Is that you, hon?" Dad called from the living room. Only the glow of the screen illuminated the room, and his face was pale in the television light. He had fallen asleep watching television. "Is something wrong?" he asked.

I jumped. "No! Nothing's wrong." I could hear my voice sounding thin and high. "Why do you ask if something's wrong?"

"Well, usually you say hello when you come in."

"I thought you were asleep." I stood on my tiptoes and peered anxiously out the small peephole in the door. No sign of anyone outside. I guessed the biker had only been trying to frighten me. If that was what he wanted, he had certainly succeeded. I took a deep breath and turned to go back to my room.

"Turning in early? Good idea," said Dad. "I may do that, too, pet. I'll be keeping early hours in the military." Dad's voice grated on me. I hadn't realized how much Mom had created Dad's image for me until she was gone. "Your dad is so proud of you," she would say, or "Your dad is a man of his word. He has real integrity." Now that she was gone, that perfect father she'd described seemed to have gone, too, and all I saw before me was this silly man who kept coming up with harebrained schemes. I wondered if he had been that way when I was little, too, and I had just never noticed. When I was in the first grade he had a workshop in the backyard where he worked on his inventions, but gradually, we had started storing bicycles and lawn equipment in the shed and by the time I was in high school I couldn't remember when he had last been back there.

Collapsing onto my bed, I realized I had left my books in the car. Too bad. Nothing could make me go outside again tonight.

Chapter 2

"Blythe! Come out here!" Dad's voice floated in the open window. I left my doughtnut on my plate and rushed out front. Dad was standing beside my car, his eyes wide with shock. My old car looked vaguely short, as if it were squatting on the driveway, and for some reason all its doors had been thrown open. I stared at it, then saw why Dad was looking at it so funny. All the tires were flat. Not just flat—there were gaping gashes in the rubber. As I got closer I could see cotton and some kind of strawlike material spilling out of the seats. The car looked pathetically vulnerable with its stuffing spilling out. I retrieved my books from the backseat and stood squeezing them tight against my chest as I gazed at the damage.

"Can you believe this?" cried Dad. "It's—it's vicious."

I didn't say anything.

"You'd better call the insurance company." Dad tugged irritably on a shirt cuff. "Since we don't have collision on this car, I'm not sure it's covered for vandalism."

I hoped it was. Four new tires weren't in the family budget. "I'd better get a ride to school," I said.

"How can you be so calm? I'm standing here literally trembling." Dad slammed the car doors closed.

"Whoever did this is sick. This is why I don't want to leave you here by yourself. There's too much of this kind of thing going on these days."

"You think people don't vandalize cars in Oregon?"

He shook his head. "I don't know what I think. I don't understand this at all."

I thought I understood it pretty well. The biker figured I almost killed him and he was getting back at me. It might not be civilized, but I did understand it. I had been stupid to let him know where I lived.

Craig D. Strathmore High School had two thousand students, which is way too many for anybody to keep track of, and everyone knew it, even the administrators. At any given time, about a tenth of the kids were skipping school. Nobody ever got caught except for Tom Fromke and Andy MacAdams who had filled their car with stolen reindeer and Santa Claus decorations before Christmas and got stopped by a cop.

The bathrooms at school were so full of smoke that I calculated using the john once probably shortened my life span by a good five months. The school had other obvious flaws, too. The yearbook staff only took pictures of their friends so a staffer's Christmas party got three pages while the school band only got one. And when it came to education, C.S.H. was not exactly one of the leading lights of the land. My biology teacher Mrs. Vipperman had been telling us to read chapter three over and over again since the second week of school. Now merchants were putting up Valentine decorations and we were still on chapter three. Mrs. Vipperman claimed she was philosophically opposed to cutting up frogs and that's why we never got any further in the book, but the real reason was that Mr. Vipperman had run off with his secretary and she was too busy plotting her revenge to make up any lesson plans. I realized this the day I found a list on the floor by the blackboard that read:

1. Hire a hit man.
2. ???

When it came to revenge, Mrs. Vipperman was short on imagination. She could have taken lessons from my biker.

Although school wasn't perfect, I wasn't complaining. I was safe there. Right now, that was enough for me.

I got a ride in to school that morning with Angela Wachtel. I sat beside her in the front seat as the ugly brick square of the main building of the school came into sight. She drove around the circular drive past kids standing in clumps and then headed for the student parking area. With a lurch the car dove down into the sharp incline to the gravel pit. At last she found a space and gave her parking brake a sharp jerk. An old Chevrolet drove past us, spraying Angela's car with gravel. Anyone who got to school as late as eight got stuck parking in the gravel-paved lower level of the student parking lot, so students with newer cars tried to arrive on campus extra early to protect their cars' finishes. This led to the unfounded rumor that a bunch of cars were permanently parked in the good places. Somebody told me in all seriousness that these cars were owned by kids who never left school and subsisted on wieners roasted over their radiators. Sometimes I believed it.

"Thanks for the ride, Angela," I said, hoisting my book bag over my shoulder.

She slammed her door shut. "Anytime. I was kind of surprised to hear from you. I would have thought if you needed a ride, you'd call Quentin." Her eyebrows rose like duplicate question marks.

"Quentin and I are kind of cooling off," I muttered.

"Oh! I didn't know."

"Neither does Quentin." Quentin Bonner and I had been a couple for over a year. Last year I thought it was true love and would last forever. What did I know? I was only fifteen. Now when I saw him, I felt slightly sick to my stomach, but the weird thing was that the old attraction hadn't completely gone away. I wasn't sure what I was going to do about the messed-up state of my life life, and I wished I hadn't mentioned it to Angela.

She hurried around the front of the car looking deeply interested. Angela and I were pretty good friends, but I wasn't ready yet to do an in-depth analysis of my feelings for Quentin. I was still too uncertain about how I felt.

"Are you interested in somebody else? Is Quentin interested in somebody else? That's it, isn't it?" She quivered with curiosity. "Quentin's interested in another girl."

"I don't want to talk about it, Angela."

"I understand. You must be devastated. I've been there. Remember when Marty dumped me? I was a zombie for weeks. And when you've gone with somebody for positively *years,* like you have, when you've been a *couple* since the word one—"

"I haven't finished my geometry yet," I said apologetically. "I've really got to run."

I bolted for my locker. But I was out of luck. Quentin was waiting for me there. It figured. As soon as I decide I'm not ready to face a problem, it's standing there waiting for me.

Quentin wore great clothes but always looked as if he had better things to think about than clothes. His eyes were blue and seemed to see things a long way off, and his two front teeth were a little bit uneven, which was the imperfection that just made you notice how very much up to par all the rest of him was. A lot of people resented his good looks. Lately, I resented them myself, but I knew it wasn't his fault he was the complete golden boy.

"Blythe, oh, love of my life. Let's go to Borneo and live on tangerines."

I twirled my combination lock, avoiding his gaze. "What's in Borneo?"

"Orangutans. I love orangutans." But already his attention had wandered. He whistled. "Hey, catch Michael Prender and Amy Johnson over there. I thought public displays of affection were strictly not allowed."

I followed his gaze then quickly looked away. Michael and Amy looked like an advertisement for Obsession. Their book bags lay forgotten at their feet.

"How's C.S.H. going to stamp out sex if they don't get any more cooperation than that?" asked Quentin, aggrieved. "Hey—Michael! Amy!"

Not surprisingly, Michael and Amy were too involved in each other to answer, but eventually he got their attention. He went right over to them, stepping over the book bags, put one hand on each of their backs, and began talking very earnestly.

I tried to pretend I didn't know him. I also tried not to hear what he said. After all, I was breaking up with him pretty soon anyway. What he was doing had nothing to do with me.

A minute later he was back, his eyes glistening with mischief. "I asked them if they were going to put out a learners' instruction manual. They're going to think it over."

Quentin could get away with things like that. It was like he owned the school. It was one of the things I used to find attractive about him. Also, he was funny and he was a straight-A student. The odd thing was that in a couple of important ways he was not too smart. I had only found that out lately.

As soon as I got my books together I smiled at him apologetically and scooted away in the direction of the girls' room. When I reached the door a cloud of smoke whooshed out to meet me. Over the sound of coughing I heard the smoke alarm. "Shut that thing off!" somebody yelled. Julie King, the basketball forward, jumped up and banged on it until it quit buzzing. I squinted my eyes into protective slits and dashed in. The girls' bathroom was the one place Quentin couldn't follow me. Looking in the mirror I practiced mouthing the words, "I think we ought to see other people." It was hard to believe I could ever say that to Quentin.

"What are you doing in here, Blythe?" coughed a girl from my homeroom. "You don't smoke."

"I don't know," I blurted. I hurried out, smelling as if I'd been barbecued.

I knew I had to get free of Quentin. My respiration still did crazy things when he leaned over me and fixed me with those cool blue eyes, but I had enough problems without having a boyfriend who made me feel almost sick with guilt for still liking him to kiss me.

Elizabeth Mattingly edged up to me. "See that boy over there? The one in the blue windbreaker? He asked me about you."

I couldn't make him out very well because there was a mob in the halls. It was so crowded that if I hadn't known better I would have suspected there had been a nasty accident in the chem lab that had cloned everybody. I was certain there had not been this many kids when school started, but then all kinds of things seemed weird to me lately. It was as if the walls were closing in on me.

All I could make out about the boy in the blue windbreaker was that he had ash-blond hair and an aquiline nose. I caught just a short flash of a look, then he was gone.

"He's new," said Elizabeth. "He asked me if you were Quentin's girlfriend."

"Tell him I'm not," I said.

Elizabeth's jaw dropped. "What?"

"Don't look at me like that, Elizabeth. People change. I'm looking for broader horizons. Understand?"

"Any boys you don't want you can toss in my direction, okay?" said Elizabeth sourly.

I had taken an important step. I hurried off to homeroom feeling almost giddy.

Chapter 3

That night, I woke up in a cold sweat. The clock dial said four and my pulse was pounding. I couldn't even remember what I had been dreaming but it must have been frightening. Nights had been bad for me ever since the accident. Days were a lot better, except that I didn't like getting in a car with Quentin anymore.

The night of the accident, it had been raining on and off all evening, but a huge crowd of kids had showed up anyway for Michael O'Hearon's party. Michael's house was halfway to the next small town. He had kegs of beer out back and a CD player going full blast. When Quentin and I were ready to go, I noticed he fumbled with his keys. "Are you all right to drive?" I asked.

"Sure. A few beers are nothing. I'm fine."

I threw my jacket over my head and made a run for the car. Quentin got in on the other side, his hair wet and plastered to his head. He started up the car, then peeled out of the driveway as if somebody had fired a starting gun. He zipped down some side streets and in a few minutes we were flying along Highway 64, heading home.

"Don't you think you ought to slow down?" I asked.

"Lay off me, Blythe. They never stop you for going five miles over the limit. Besides, this baby can stop on a dime."

I had only had my license a few months. I don't think I realized that nobody can stop on a dime when they're going sixty miles an hour. Particularly when they've had a few beers and it's raining. Quentin picked up a tape and snapped it into the tape player. The windows fogged up. I was rubbing my palm over my side to clear the window when I saw red taillights too close ahead. Someone had pulled out in front of us.

"Watch out!" I shrieked.

Quentin slammed on the brakes but it was too late. The car hydroplaned. In the split second, the freeze-frame of awareness before we hit, I was sure I was going to die. There was no time for any other thought as the tons of metal in the two vehicles crushed together. They skidded together for a while, obscenely locked, and then stopped. I realized that against all odds, I was still alive. I glanced over at Quentin. Tears were pouring down his cheeks in shiny streaks and he was making animal-like whimpering noises. The windshield was a spider web of broken glass with red light reflecting in it. The sharp smell of gasoline filled my nostrils and I heard people yelling outside. It occurred to me that the car might explode, but I couldn't move. What had been the frame of the door on my side was bent against me and the glove compartment was pressing against my legs. I thought about all the movies I'd seen of cars bursting into flames and terror rose in me like nausea.

The door on Quentin's side was thrown open and a fat man with a shiny, worried face stuck his head in. "Are you okay? Come on, son, let's get you out." He put his hands under Quentin's arms and dragged him out of the car. I sensed other people were standing behind him, dark shapes I could just make out. "Okay, what about you, girlie?" The man sounded desperate. "Can you move your legs?"

I swallowed hard and wiggled my toes. I knew then that my legs were okay. If I could only get out of the car before it exploded I would be all right. "If you give me a tug, I think I can get out." I gritted my teeth.

"You sure your legs aren't hurt?"

"I'm fine but I don't have any room to move. I'm stuck."

The good samaritan pushed the seat release and slid the seat back another inch, then he reached over and pulled me out across the seat. He smelled strongly of cigars and hair tonic, but I'd never been so glad to be in anybody's arms in my life. When he stood me up on my wobbly legs, I saw that there was nothing left of the hood of Quentin's car but a battery that dangled precariously from a mass of crushed metal. Even more grotesquely, the car looked as if it had eaten up the smaller one we had hit. It had climbed up the other car and the other car's top had buckled.

"You better stand clear, girlie. Can you stand up okay? Maybe you better sit down," said the fat man.

A couple of cops had Quentin. Flashing lights were everywhere around us now. It took a while for it to dawn on me that one of the cars was an ambulance. "Is that for us?" I asked. I was still dazed.

A man in a sweatshirt said nervously. "Nope, that's for the girl in the other car."

I haltingly walked over toward the ambulance and I saw her lying on the rolling stretcher, blood on her face. She was a beautiful girl about my age with blond hair that streamed over her shoulders and I wanted to think she was going to be all right, but I knew she wouldn't. She looked like a broken doll, a beautiful china doll with white skin. Maybe she was so white because she had already bled a lot.

I backed away hastily as they slid her into the ambulance. I had a cold, sick feeling in the bottom my stomach when I realized that what had happened was partly my fault. I should have stopped Quentin from driving. I should have taken the keys away from him and called his parents.

That was what I thought about late at night when I lay in bed. I was having a lot of trouble sleeping.

They didn't even take Quentin's license away. He hadn't been legally drunk, he'd just had enough of a rosy glow to make him imagine he could stop on a dime in the rain. They charged him with driving too fast for conditions and a lot of people at school felt sorry for him. Quentin's friends kept saying that it had been awful weather that night and that accidents happen.

The girl in the other car went to Southwest Enderby County High, fifteen miles away, so none of us knew her or had to feel sorry for her. She didn't seem to count much next to Quentin. A few days after the accident, Quentin went to see her in the hospital. I had to give him credit for that because I wouldn't have had the nerve.

He came over to my house afterwards and took my hands in his and I could tell he was cold all over. "Blythe, they say she's never going to be able to walk again without help." His face crumpled.

I thought about what it would be like to be perfectly okay one second and have your life come undone in a split second, and I felt sick.

"Turns out she wanted to be a dancer. God, my hands are shaking—look at them." We sat in silence for a long while. I didn't know what to say. Quentin jumped up and paced the floor. "Come on. God, I've got to snap out of this or I'm going to go crazy. I've got to get my mind off of it somehow. Let's go get some hamburgers."

I drew away from him. "I've got to write my history paper."

"You can do that later," he said irritably. "Can't you see I need some company?"

I went with him. We got hamburgers.

What bothered me was that a week later Quentin was just fine. I kept picturing the girl struggling along in therapy somewhere, trying to learn to use a walker or a wheelchair.

I wished I hadn't seen her and wished Quentin hadn't told me she'd planned to be a dancer. Sometimes her face came to me strongly in my dreams.

Quentin didn't mention the accident again, but I couldn't forget it. As soon as he put his arm around me and I began to feel that old attraction, I felt waves of guilt. It was way too much for me to handle.

I think that was why when Elizabeth pointed out the boy in the blue windbreaker, I was so interested. Intuitively I sensed I could use him to help me get free of Quentin.

By Monday, I had new tires on my car. Dad put them on his charge card. I had tried to mend the seat cushions with clear plastic tape but it was hopeless. I would have to try something else—maybe nylon stretch seat covers. But now that the car was fixed at least I could get to school on my own.

Quentin spotted me pulling into the lot and yelled

hi. He skated down the gravelly incline in his Reeboks like he was surfing, never once losing his balance, and sauntered over to my car. He couldn't just walk, he had to go in style. "I've got a new idea for a little business I can open on the side," he announced. "Flowers by Bubba. Master stroke, huh? I cash in on the yuppie clientele and get the pickup truck crowd, too."

"I don't think people called Bubba buy flowers."

"Details, babe, details." He had his left arm around me and his book bag slung over one shoulder and he still had his right hand free for greeting his friends. "How's it going Benj?" He gave a broad wave and a smile, like he was running for class president.

"Quentin?" I lowered my voice so he had to bend down to hear me. "Quentin, don't you ever think about that girl who was hurt in the accident?"

The blood drained from his face. "Sure, Blythe. Heck, I think about it all the time, but accidents happen. Nobody hates it more than me, but it's over. It's done." He licked his lips.

A loud whoop from the other end of the hall almost made me drop my books. Biff jumped up and smacked his hand against the wall. "Heya, Quent, old man! Come here. Got something for you."

"Gotta go," said Quentin hastily. "Biff owes me five bucks. I'd better not let him get away."

I watched Quentin gallop away down the hall. Maybe he was right. I was getting morbid.

Then that afternoon, when I went out to the parking lot after school, everything was different. The boy in the blue windbreaker was waiting for me. He was leaning on my car, a brave guy since lots of people would have had serious doubts whether my car could stand their weight.

"Interesting car you got here." He smiled.

"Thank you. It has its own personality."

He peered in the window on the driver's side. "Sort of spilling its guts out, though, isn't it?"

"It had a nasty accident. Somebody came after it with a knife."

He whistled. "You must be a lady with serious enemies."

"No. It was just mindless vandalism." Somehow I didn't want to tell anyone about the biker. I was still pretending to myself that I had imagined the dark figure that had followed me home.

"I'm glad it wasn't an enemy of yours, because I'm a certified coward and I'd want to stand clear if a hit man was gunning for you."

His clothes were different; not exactly weird, just different from what we wear at Strathmore High. His sneakers were a different brand, and he had a black bandanna tied around one knee of his jeans. His flannel shirt was tied around his waist and his top four tee-shirt buttons were undone, even though the weather was cool. His fair hair seemed to have a life of its own. It fell over his forehead and left his slate-gray eyes in shadow. He looked different from anyone I'd ever known, yet somehow oddly familiar in a way that made me uncomfortable.

"I think we're neighbors," he said.

I was startled. "How do you know where I live?" For a second I got deep into paranoia and wondered if he was the biker.

"Recognized your car," he said.

I had to admit that my car was pretty distinctive. It still showed the three different colors of the three cars it had been made from, which gave it an offbeat look. I took out my keys. "Where did you say you live?"

"We're not actually in your subdivision," he explained. "I live a bit down the road."

"But there isn't anything farther down the road except—"

"Yup, that's it. That's where I live."

"The Croger mansion?" I stared. "Are you the ones that put up the big fence around the whole property? What's that about? Are you that worried about somebody trying to sell you magazine subscriptions?"

"The fence is just because of the animals. My dad and his partner use animals in their act."

I thought about the tall, painted iron fence. Whatever they were keeping in there it wasn't gerbils. "Are they lion tamers?"

He laughed. "Nah. They're magicians. Mostly they play Las Vegas. They're booked there six months out of the year. But they thought this would be as good a place as any to work up their new acts. I used to live out in the country with my mom, but now I'm living with my dad. You should come over sometime and let me show you around. The mansion takes some getting used to. It's quite a—well, to tell you the truth, it's kind of overdone." Big grin.

"I'd like to see it," I said. This was true. I'd never been inside a spooky three-story mansion owned by a magician. It sounded interesting, to say the very least.

"I'm counting on it," he said. "Come on out and I'll give you the grand tour." I was used to Quentin's splashy entrances and exits; this boy slipped away almost before I realized it, and I hadn't remembered to ask his name.

I wrenched open the door and got into my car.

During the exodus of cars from the gravel pit, I had a lot to think about. The guy with the slate-gray eyes was obviously interested in me. He had asked Elizabeth if I was Quentin's girlfriend and then he had taken the trouble to find which car was mine and had waited for me. I was intrigued.

I didn't kid myself, though. A big part of my interest in him was that he might be a short-term solution to my problem with Quentin. I was having a tough time persuading myself, much less Quentin, that I didn't love him anymore since it was only half-true. Maybe if I started going out with another guy—well, actions speak louder than words.

I drove toward home. After a while I saw the Holmhaven sign ahead on the left. On an impulse I didn't turn in but kept going. I drove on through the woods about a mile and a half past our turn before I spotted the green painted iron fence. It must have been all of eight feet high. I remember when Dad and I had talked about getting a dinky little chain-link fence around our yard but even that cost too much. This tall iron fence was more the sort of thing they throw around Buckingham Palace and probably cost a fortune. The magician business must pay well. I pulled the car over to the side and looked down the roadway that led to the house. The house wasn't visible from the road, too many trees in the way, but I could see its three dark towers outlined against the sky. The expense of heating, cooling, and painting it must be awful. I bet the real estate company had a celebration when it sold.

As I gazed curiously at the dark towers of the house outlined against the colorless sky, a crow wheeled over the trees, banked on the curve, and then with a hoarse croak sank into the black silhouette of a tree. Even after I got in my car and drove home, I kept remembering the towers of the house jutting ominously above the trees. Not that looking at the place had told me much about the boy with the gray eyes.

Chapter 4

The boy with the gray eyes was called Harry, I found out from Elizabeth the next day. She wasn't too sure of his last name. Willard, Wolford, she hazarded. Or maybe it was Hensley. Big help she was.

My heart was doing crazy things out of sheer excitement as I walked to my car after school. I was certain Harry would be waiting there for me. He wasn't. Instead, next to my car a couple of football players squatted behind a beat-up Plymouth drawing lines in the gravel. Something to do with football plays, I supposed. A fine cloud of dust rose over the gravel as cars varoomed out of the lot. Marsha Fenton glanced at me and got a fit of the giggles, which didn't do a lot for my poise. I smoothed my hair self-consciously and looked around, hoping to see Harry. I felt stupid standing there waiting for him. My feet felt as big as snowshoes and I started worrying that a place on my chin felt warm, as if a pimple was about to pop out.

Quentin's little white Toyota skidded to a stop next to me, spraying gravel with unerring aim against my legs. Quentin poked his head out the window. "Pick you up at nine, okay?"

"Sure. Fine," I said.

He sped off leaving me choking on exhaust fumes.

The Sweetheart Dance had been on my schedule for so long that I had almost quit paying attention to the pink heart I had drawn around the date on the calendar. It was the best dance of the year. No gym mats in the corner and no basketball hoops over the punch bowl because it was always held at the Yacht Club, which was swankier than the Silver Brook Club. Silver Brook was for people who wanted to swim and play golf whereas the Yacht Club was for expense accounts and girls having debutante parties. There, swimming and golf were merely footnotes to the important activities.

The dance was sponsored by C.S.H.'s two illegal fraternities, the Paladins and the Green Cheese Club. Quentin said we had to go because he was president of the Paladins but that wasn't exactly true. The truth was he loved every minute of it and only pretended that he was forced to go. Give him a punch bowl and a boutonniere and put him in the center of the action and he was divinely happy. If the Paladins had told him he didn't have to bother to come, he'd have been sick.

I was going to have to wear the same dress I'd worn the year before, but my rose satin was simple, not flashy, and I figured nobody would remember that they'd seen it before. What was bothering me was not the dress but that I wasn't looking forward to dancing cheek to cheek with Quentin. I wasn't even up to holding hands.

So after Quentin drove off, I stood there in the parking lot, dreading the whole thing. I was also half-ready to cry. I felt as if I'd been abandoned by Harry. Where *was* he? He was supposed to solve my problem. After all, he had more than implied that he expected to be around in my future. It hadn't been precisely stated, but it was there in the subtext all right. He had a nerve to leave me standing in the parking lot breathing Quentin's exhaust! After thinking a while about what a creep he was to let me down, I was really steamed. I would have slammed my car door when I got in except that I was afraid it might fall off. So I closed it firmly but carefully and drove home. This time when I saw the Holmhaven sign that marked our neighborhood, I didn't drive on to take a peek at the mansion. After the way Harry had stood me up, not a chance was I going to park and peer at the mansion from a distance. I was getting very neurotic and worried that he might be up in a turret with a pair of binoculars watching me and having a good laugh.

I didn't have any rational reason to be mad at Harry because he hadn't actually promised he would meet me at the parking lot, but I wasn't looking at it rationally. I couldn't stand it that everything was back to normal and I was going to the Sweetheart Dance with Quentin after all. I decided it was all Harry's fault.

That night when Quentin showed up at the house, scrubbed shiny and bright, I was nervously checking my hair in the hall mirror. I hated seeing him all keyed up and ready to party. It reminded me too much of the night of Michael O'Hearon's party.

"Honey, look! Look what Quentin's brought you!" Dad cried.

I turned around and saw Quentin whip out from behind his back an old-fashioned posy. Baby pink carnations were tightly bound into a bouquet with a white lace doily wrapped around it like a frilly collar. As a corsage it was screamingly impractical. It looked as if it had jumped off of an old-fashioned valentine. "Do I pin it on, or what?" I asked.

"You hold it in your dainty hand when you go to meet your sweetheart," crowed Quentin. He held out a crooked arm for me to hang onto. "That's me—your sweetheart."

A world where people lived out their whole lives in denim and sweatshirts didn't give Quentin the scope he needed. I knew that and for Christmas I had given him a sterling-silver pen knife engraved with his initials. It came from Tiffany's in a baby blue box tied up with white ribbon and was tiny enough to put on a key ring. It was just his kind of thing—special, expensive, and elegant.

I tucked the small bouquet in my belt and took his arm. "Bye, Dad."

"Let me get a picture before you go, kids," said Dad.

Quentin and I stood there in the hall with rictus smiles on our faces while Dad fired off the camera. This was standard procedure at our house. I would probably get confused and disoriented if I ever left for a dance without blue dots in front of my eyes.

"Your steed, milady." Outside, Quentin flung open the car door for me. Then he trotted around to the other side and got in himself.

Quentin hit the gas at once, taking off with a jack-rabbit start that left us both with incipient whiplash. Once we got out on the highway, he restlessly flexed his hands on the steering wheel. His eyes sparkled and I could see he was already gearing up to a higher key for the party. He kept shifting in and out of lanes as if no lane was quite good enough or fast enough. "Biff told me he got a special act to fill in when the deejay takes a break," he said. "It was my idea, actually. I helped with the decorations, too. We decided to go with a black-magic theme." He threw me a quick, sheepish glance.

"It's okay, Quentin. We all know you hated every minute of it."

He laughed. "Okay, so I really get off on parties. So, sue me. The trouble is you know me too well, Blythe." He grinned that twenty-four-karat grin of his, self-mocking and charming. So—why not? I thought. Since when is being charming a crime?

The tailights of the car ahead of us were reflected in the chrome on Quentin's hood; we were that close to the other guy. I bit my lip, but not so hard that I actually drew blood. I was trying to get a grip. It seemed like the best plan under the circumstances.

The whole time we were on the road I was tense from head to toe, but we didn't crash. We didn't even come close. Instead, a few minutes later we turned smoothly into the circular driveway in front of the Yacht Club. Tiny twinkle lights studded the trees. Music poured out the door. Kids were leaving their cars and walking together in couples toward the entrance. The parking lot was already full and people were having to park along the street. It turned out Quentin knew of a parking space back by the service entrance, half-hidden by the dumpster and a brick wall, and he pulled his car into that. He always managed to get an edge somehow.

The doors to the ballroom were flanked by big pots of some kind of white flower, and a crowd was dancing inside. Quentin liked to arrive after things had gotten underway but before people had started to wonder if he was going to show up. The deejay was playing an old song, "Black Magic Woman," which I guess was supposed to underscore the theme of the dance because I heard it again later. Twinkle lights were threaded into white crepe paper flowers that were scattered everywhere, and since the walls were mirrored, the lights and flowers were multiplied in the reflection. I had the sensation of being lost in a sea of twinkle lights, which was a little disorienting at first. I had to focus on the floor until I got my bearings. Then I took a look around—girls I had never seen except in jeans were dressed in poufed satin dresses and all the guys were in their Sunday suits and sneakers, which was as close as anybody at our school came to a personal fashion statement.

Matt Milner, who was president of the Green Cheese Club, poked Quentin in the ribs. "You're late, man. I thought you'd wrecked your car again."

Quentin's face darkened and I took a quick step back, not wanting to see the anger in his eyes. I knew it was the last thing he wanted to be reminded of. He probably figured Matt was getting at him on purpose. It was hard for Quentin to grasp that most of the time people weren't so much malicious as just plain stupid.

Quentin managed to swallow his anger, but his voice was tight when he spoke. "Guess you haven't heard that the party doesn't start till I get here."

"Yeah, right," said Matt. "Get yourself some punch, man. I hear the deejay's gonna take his break any minute."

Quentin steered me over to the punch bowl. "It's hot enough in here. Where does Matt get off telling me I'm late? Is he my mother all of a sudden? And that crack about my car wreck. He's got a nerve."

The punch was not spiked. It was not that kind of party. Quentin had once explained to me very earnestly that anybody could go over to somebody's backyard and get drunk every weekend, but only the Paladins and the Green Cheese Club could put on a dance that had real glamor.

I cradled my punch cup in my hands and looked around. It gave me a funny feeling in my stomach when I realized that unconsciously I was scanning the crowd for Harry, even though there was no chance Harry was a member of either the Paladins or the Green Cheese Club. Members got tapped for both clubs before school in the tenth grade. It was a big deal which unofficially christened the most popular boys in the school. When I caught myself looking around for Harry, I felt dumb.

The deejay was talking so fast I couldn't make out what he was saying, but suddenly there was a roll of drums and the stage curtains jerkily pulled open. I blinked and stared. Unsmiling, in the middle of the stage, wearing a black tuxedo and a red-lined satin evening cape, stood Harry. Everybody in the ballroom applauded. Standing next to Harry was an elaborate old-fashioned cabinet and at the back of the stage on the other side was a spiral staircase painted gold and spangled with glitter. It looked like part of the set for an old Fred Astaire movie. The stairs spiraled once and then ended in thin air. Clearly they were only for dancing upon.

"This is it," hissed Quentin. "The special act they're going to do while the deejay takes his break. Remember? My idea?"

Music played that reminded me of a circus. I half-expected clowns to run out on stage, but Harry stood there alone, very soberly, next to what looked like an old-fashioned record cabinet. I assumed he was playing taped music of his own on a concealed boom box. He ostentatiously adjusted his bow tie, swept off his top hat, then placed it behind the cabinet. He pushed up his cuffs to show us that nothing was hidden there and began pulling chiffon scarves out of his sleeve. People tittered. It seemed that miles and miles of scarves were coming out. There was no end to them. But finally, the stitched-together scarves lay like melted sherbet on the floor in front of him. He looked up with a pleased smile and clapped his hands in the air. The boom box made a large bang and there was a flash in the air. Everyone gasped at the noise. Then he reached to retrieve his hat, mimed surprised, and pulled a rabbit out of the hat. An actual rabbit. It made a few tentative hops around the stage while everybody roared with laughter. Harry picked it up, put it inside the cabinet, and closed the door.

"How did he do that?" I asked. "You don't think he had the rabbit inside when it was on his head, do you?"

"Probably two identical hats behind the cabinet," said Quentin. "Magic tricks are usually simple. They just divert your eye for a second. It's easy. It's all showmanship. But he's good, don't you think?" Quentin beamed as if he'd invented Harry.

Next Harry opened the doors of the cabinet to show that the rabbit was still there, then closed it while martial music played. When he opened the cabinet the second time the rabbit jumped out. And then another rabbit. Four rabbits hopped out and were soon softly loping around the stage.

"There must be a false back to the cabinet," said Quentin.

"Don't tell me how it works," I said. "You spoil it."

I was enchanted. I wasn't sure how much of what charmed me was the act and how much was Harry. A couple of kids nearby clambered up the stage and helped Harry catch all the rabbits. As soon as the rabbits were back in the cabinet, coins began showering out of Harry's sleeve to his evident surprise. He looked puzzled, took off his shoes, and began pouring gold coins out of them.

Then, still looking slightly embarrassed, he began going up the spiral staircase in his stocking feet. I held my breath, hoping that the glitzy steps were solidly constructed. They went up to at least twice Harry's height and had no railing.

Quentin winced. "This is where I can't look," he whispered.

Quentin didn't like people to know, but he had a thing about heights. He had never been on a ferris wheel in his life. He told me once that he never even climbed trees when he was little.

As Harry continued his surefooted ascent on the star-studded staircase, it seemed yet another proof of his natural superiority over Quentin. When he reached the top of the staircase, the music stopped and all eyes were on him as he wrapped his cape over his face. Suddenly there was a series of pops and clouds as swirling smoke engulfed the top of the staircase. I could hear gasps all over the ballroom. When the smoke cleared, Harry was gone.

"Let's hear it for the magician, folks!" yelled the deejay. Thunderous applause. Harry limped back onstage in his stocking feet. He bowed once with a rueful smile, picked up his shoes, and then slipped offstage while we were all still applauding.

The deejay put on something loud that I didn't recognize and people began dancing.

"That seemed to go over pretty well, didn't it?"

said Quentin. "Did I mention more than six or eight times that it was my idea?"

"It was incredible!" I cried. "All that colored smoke! I mean, this was no amateur act. How did you even know about him?" I asked.

"Biff got him, as a matter of fact. I think the guy did some demonstration in class or something and Biff saw it. But it was my idea that we have some kind of act this year. And of course, the theme was black magic so that gave us the idea of getting a magician. Trouble was nobody knew where to get one but then Biff remembered this guy did card tricks and asked him."

Even though we were dancing, Quentin couldn't stop himself from looking over my shoulder, saying hi to his friends and checking out the other girls. "Jeez, look at Elizabeth in that dress," he muttered. "She looks like a sausage. Hey-ey! Hiya, Elizabeth, Biff. Great magician, huh?"

"They do it with mirrors," said Biff solemnly.

Elizabeth tittered.

Quentin wheeled me into a double turn. "Good old Biff, always trying to be funny. Too bad he can never quite pull it off."

Harry was over by the punch bowl, but I couldn't figure out how to get away from Quentin and go speak to him. I saw Matt bearing down on us with a look of determination, his face shiny and his boutonniere slightly crushed. This was my chance to escape. "Here comes Matt," I said. "While you two talk about club business, I'm going to get some punch." Quentin didn't protest as I slipped away. He took me for granted. That must have been why he hadn't even noticed that things weren't right between us.

I pushed my way through the crowd, and when I

got to the punch bowl, I was breathless. Harry's startlingly white shirt made a thin triangle that seemed to point to his face. His bow tie, now untied, hung limp from his collar. I picked up one of the tepid cups of punch lined up on the white tablecloth and slurped some on my dress. Luckily the color matched. I put it down hastily. My hands weren't steady enough for drinking punch. "Great show," I said awkwardly. "I mean, you're really good."

"Thanks," he said. "Hot enough in here, isn't it?" He upended a glass and gulped down more punch.

I threw a glance over my shoulder. In the crowd I couldn't see Quentin, which was just as well. I felt guilty enough as it was. "The club has got a terrace," I said. "It'll be cooler out there."

Harry refilled his punch glass. "Want to get a breath of fresh air?"

"Okay," I said uncertainly. "Let's do that."

Harry didn't know the way so I had to lead. The doors to the terrace were in the dining room next to the ballroom. The tables were bare and the light was dim in there now that dinner was over. I pushed open the curtained doors to the terrace. On summer evenings the doors were thrown open and tables with candles were put out on the terrace. But this was no summer evening and tonight a cold blast hit us. Harry let the door swing shut behind us and the sound of the music was suddenly muffled. A few limp evergreen bushes bordered the paved terrace blocking what in daytime would be a broad vista of the golf course. It was not really dark on the terrace because the curtained windows of the ballroom let through light but it was plenty cold and I shivered. Harry slid off his cape and handed it to me. He fumbled with the pocket of his jacket a minute as I snuggled into the cape gratefully. A flare of light made me look up at him. He had lit a match. He sucked on a cigarette then tossed the spent match away. Its red tip glowed for an instant on the paving stone. I didn't let on, but I was surprised that he was smoking. I didn't think I knew anyone else who did. The light of the cigarette shone bright for an instant and then ebbed to a dull glow. I decided this was probably not the moment to mention the health warnings on the cigarette package.

"Your act was really incredible," I said. "Did your dad teach you how to do all that stuff?"

"It's basic stuff." He shrugged. "My dad and his partner have an act that's—well, it's on a much bigger scale. What I do is just for fun."

"Everybody loved it." I hesitated. "I thought maybe I'd see you at the parking lot this afternoon." I stopped. The last thing I wanted to do was to give him the idea I had nothing better to do than wait around for him. I had already made that mistake once with Quentin.

"Are you saying you missed me?" He smiled. "Great!"

"I didn't exactly miss you," I amended. "It's just that I expected to see you there. You know how you run into the same people again and again." I shrugged.

Harry smiled. "So, what's happened to the boyfriend?"

I shot an anxious glance toward the ballroom. "He had to talk about club business, I think. I said I'd go get some punch because it was really hot in there."

"How does the boyfriend feel about you going out with other guys?"

I shook my hair loose from the collar of Harry's cape. "He doesn't own me."

"Somebody told me you two had been going together for years and I thought maybe—"

"Ancient history," I said firmly.

He threw his cigarette to the pavement. It swirled in a tight little circle then lay glowing on the stone. "That's encouraging," he said. He ground the butt under his heel deliberately and I wondered why he was throwing it away when it wasn't even half-finished. Then he pulled me toward him and pressed his lips against mine. I could sense his warmth and taste the smoke that clung to his lips.

"Want to go get pizza tomorrow night?" he whispered.

"Sounds thrilling."

"You've got it backwards." He grinned. "I'm thrilling. The pizza just tastes good."

I was so startled I backed off and stared at him a moment without my expression changing. It was the sort of thing Quentin might have said.

"Are you okay?" he asked anxiously. "Did I say something wrong?"

I shook my head. "No, everything's great. So, uh, what's your name?"

He laughed. "I guess I ought to mention that, huh? Harry Weaver. Harry R. Weaver, actually, but I never tell anybody what the R. stands for, so don't ask."

"Rastus?" I guessed. "Rapunzel? Rumpelstiltskin!"

"I'm sorry I brought it up. Can I take you home before we die of frostbite or do you have to get back to your boyfriend?"

Another couple came out the door. The girl looked vaguely familiar but I didn't know the boy. They obviously had expected to be alone and didn't look a bit pleased to see us.

"I better get back," I said. I was afraid Quentin

was going to be wondering where I was. One part of my mind thought that if I wanted to break off with him then a quick and easy way to do it would be to stay out on the terrace kissing Harry until he came looking for me, but another part of me shrank from the scene. The grown-up thing to do would be to simply tell him I wanted to see other people. But I wasn't having much success bringing up the subject. Unfounded rumor would be a good first step. Then when Quentin accused me of sneaking around on him, I could, ever so reluctantly, admit the truth.

We slipped past the couple locked in a passionate embrace. Inside, the heat and the noise hit us like a blast. Harry was still pale with the cold. I gave him back his cape and thanked him.

"I won't have any trouble finding your house tomorrow, will I?" He rubbed his hands together briskly.

"I don't think so. My car will be parked out in front and it's pretty unmistakable. The genuine article—accept no substitutes."

"I wouldn't think of it." He smiled slightly, meeting my eyes. "You're the only one that will do."

Hot color rushed to my face and I was glad to turn away from him. I pushed my way into the crowd in the ballroom, pressing ahead swiftly, and a minute later I felt comfortingly anonymous. I had already lost sight of Harry. Quentin and I had been going together so long I was a little vague about normal first-date behavior, but it seemed to me that something along the lines of "Have you read any good books lately?" ought to come before "You're the only one." I was warm with embarrassment and I wondered momentarily if I was getting into this thing with Harry a bit too quickly.

Suddenly Quentin took me by the shoulders. "Where the heck have you been, Blythe? I've been looking everywhere for you. I was about to get Elizabeth to check the ladies' room. I felt like an idiot going around asking everybody if they'd seen you. Where've you been?"

I knew I couldn't have been gone for more than a few minutes. In my opinion Quentin was carrying possessiveness to a ridiculous extreme. "I went out to get a breath of fresh air," I said.

"You went out on the terrace?" Quentin chortled. "What're you really up to? Taking pictures of the passion pit for the yearbook?"

"Do you want to dance or what?" I said coldly.

"Sure. Let's dance."

Later on, I saw Elizabeth looking at me. She whispered something to Biff behind her hand and I knew the rumor mill was already in gear. It wouldn't be long until Quentin found out what I had been doing on the terrace.

Chapter 5

I was green with fatigue when Quentin finally agreed to leave the party. He disappeared down the hall to fetch my coat from the cloakroom.

"This is always such a great dance," crooned Elizabeth. "I just love the black-magic theme." Her brilliant blue dress was ruched so tightly that I could see why Quentin had said she looked like a sausage. She shot me a sly glance. "You feel almost anything could happen tonight with all this romance in the air and all the secret corners and hidey places around the club. Some people just might—well, lose it, do something they'd really regret later on, you know what I'm saying?"

Obviously, somehow or other she had heard about me kissing Harry out on the terrace. I longed to assure her that I didn't regret a thing, but that would only confirm the rumor, and I didn't want to give her the satisfaction.

I was sort of surprised that she had come with Biff. So far as I knew they didn't go together. I had expected Biff to have better taste. When he showed up with her coat, Elizabeth beamed at him. "See ya later," Biff said uncomfortably. They pushed open the double glass doors and disappeared into the night.

A heartbeat later Quentin appeared, and I noticed

he was white around the lips. He and Biff had to have been talking in the cloakroom. Just for a second I regretted that kiss on the terrace. Quentin helped me into my coat and silently pushed the door open for me. I was already tensing for the inevitable explosion. I stepped out onto the brick steps, catching my breath a little with the cold as a breeze brushed my face. Across the street a few lights from distant houses twinkled icily through the woods.

When we got to the car Quentin unlocked my door and waited while I got in. Then he slid in behind the wheel. "So what's this Biff tells me about you making out with the magician guy out on the terrace?" he said.

"I wasn't making out with him!"

He relaxed. "I told Biff he had it all wrong—" he began.

Suddenly I remembered. I was supposed to be breaking up with Quentin. "Actually, Harry is kind of interesting. I enjoyed talking with him," I said quickly.

"Dammit, Blythe, what's going on? Are you trying to make me jealous?"

"I like him. We're going out tomorrow night."

"You don't even *know* him. Are you out of your mind?" He was staring at me in amazement.

"Strange as it may seem, there are reasons I might want to go out with another guy besides being out of my mind."

"I don't want you to go out with other guys," he said. "You're my girl."

"I'm not sure I want to be your girl, Quentin. I—I need some space. I think we both ought to see other people."

Quentin tore out of the parking place and narrowly missed clipping the fender of a parked Mercedes.

"You're driving like a maniac," I said.

"I'm upset." His tires squealed as he braked for the stop sign. "Anybody would be upset. I go to the dance expecting to have a great time and all of a sudden you start jerking me around."

"Well, pull yourself together before you get us in another wreck."

He winced as if burned.

"I think we should quit seeing each other," I said. "It's not the end of the world. People break up all the time."

"Not with me, they don't." His foot bore down on the accelerator. Normally I would have been frightened, but to my surprise I felt a strange calm. I guess speed felt right because in a way I was gunning my own internal accelerator. I knew I had to or I would get sucked back into the relationship. I needed a very strong push to get free of Quentin because in spite of everything I still liked him a lot.

"I don't want to fight with you, Blythe," he said between gritted teeth. "Let's just forget everything that happened tonight, okay?"

"I don't want to forget it," I said stubbornly. "I want to go out with Harry."

"Who's even heard of this guy?" he exploded. "He's nothing."

"I didn't expect you to understand."

"You know what? This is a phase you're going through. That's what it is. You just want to experiment, play around some. You've got this fantasy of being a free spirit or something."

"No," I said. "That's not true."

There was a long silence and then it seemed to occur to him that he might be making a mistake in yelling at me.

"Why don't we go to Topps," he said, shooting an anxious glance my way. "We'll get something to eat and talk this out. Okay? Maybe I—I guess you think I take you for granted, or something like that."

"I wish you would take me home. I'm awfully tired."

"Okay." His eyes were uneasy. "Look, I'll call you tomorrow, okay?"

"Don't."

"Okay, I'll give you some time to think about it. And then I'll call you."

I didn't answer, and when Quentin dropped me off I walked into the house without even glancing back. I felt noble, like George Washington in the picture where he's crossing the Delaware. Dad was asleep in front of the television as usual and awoke with a jerk. "Hi, sweetheart. Did you have a nice time?"

I made a sort of indeterminate noise which he took for agreement. He yawned. "PBS is doing a three part special on the Kalahari desert."

Quentin loved that stuff—the nomads, the flowing robes, and the horses appealed to his romantic streak. I was thinking that I would have to mention the PBS series to him. I guess it hadn't yet sunk in that we had broken up.

I kept expecting to hear from Quentin, so all the next day I was mentally rehearsing lines about needing more space and wanting to remain friends. I didn't get to use them because he didn't call. Most of the afternoon I spent sprawled on the living room floor, leafing through the comics and wondering if I'd made a big mistake.

Dad was sitting in the hall surrounded by boxes of clothes and books. The government was supposed to issue him what he needed, but he was compulsively sorting through his belongings anyway. It was some weird version of a farewell ceremony, I guess.

He got teary-eyed over the stacks of old photographs and letters. Which picture of Mom should he take? he asked me plaintively—the one of her when they got married or the one taken just a couple of years ago where she looks thin and tired? Should he take a picture of me as a four-year-old in a sunbonnet or my last year's school picture which made me look like a fugitive from justice? Unspoken was the understanding that for us the good times had happened long ago.

He was having a lot of trouble choosing a book that would be good company for him if bombs exploded around his ears. "I can't decide whether I want to be stuck in a foxhole with *Tristram Shandy* or with *Moby Dick,*" he said.

"I'd forget the book and take sunscreen, if I were you," I said. "And extra safety pins, maybe. Safety pins always come in handy. I remember that from camp."

A few hours later Harry showed up. When I introduced him, Dad looked confused. I realized that maybe I should have mentioned that I had broken up with Quentin because it couldn't have been more obvious that Dad was frantically trying to figure out where Harry fit into the picture.

It was great to be getting out of the house. Sitting around all day waiting for the phone to ring was starting to get to me.

When we got to the car, Harry looked me over and

pursed his lips in appreciation. "You look terrific," he said. "I guess guys tell you that all the time."

I smiled at him. "I can't hear it enough." Actually, I had made an extra effort. I was wearing my shortest flip of a skirt, Daring Red nail polish, and industrial-strength eye makeup.

We drove to the mall and parked on the cinema side. Several couples in the line outside the movie swiveled their heads around to look at us. I was surprised to see that their heads seemed to have perfect circular mobility, like owls. Obviously they were registering shock that I wasn't with Quentin. Luckily, Harry seemed to be unaware of the attention we were getting. "You like buttered popcorn?" he asked. I nodded. He joined the mob in front of the popcorn machine and I lost sight of him. For a second I got the panicky feeling that I had forgotten what he looked like and that maybe I wouldn't recognize him when he came back. But then he appeared, smiling and precariously balancing the tub of popcorn between two drinks. I appraised him critically. He was fine-boned, slender, and certainly not the first person you noticed in the room. He was rather colorless, with those gray eyes and ash-blond hair. And not nearly as tall as Quentin. But there was something about him, hard to pin down but nevertheless quite attractive. Maybe it was only that I couldn't guess what he was thinking, which made him seem grown up, but I found myself drawn to him. "Maybe we'd better sit down," he suggested. We pushed the swinging doors to the theater open and felt our way in the darkness to our seats.

The movie turned out to be dumb, but that was okay with me because I was ready for some comic relief. Afterwards we went to Topps, which was the place everybody from school went to hang out. The fact that the health department had closed the place a couple of times just added to its charm. Smoke from burned grease and the smell of horseradish hung in a faint blue haze in the air. Brown leatherette booths with split seat cushions, brown paneled walls, and linoleum floors that were worn down to the bare wood at a spot in front of the cash register were what passed for interior decoration. The usual overflow crowd was stuffed into the place but we were lucky and got a booth as some people were leaving.

"So, how's old Quentin taking being dumped?" Harry asked as we sat down.

"I didn't dump him," I said. "We both decided it would be good for us to see other people." The lie was automatic and I flushed uncomfortably when I realized that it seemed to be an instinct for me to protect Quentin.

To my relief the conversation soon turned away from Quentin and instead toward Harry's problems with algebra. Personally, I love algebra. I love its tidiness and the way you can start with a bunch of x's and end up with answers.

"Maybe I could help out," I said. "I've done some algebra tutoring. Normally, I get five dollars an hour." Actually, what I usually got was four dollars an hour, but with Dad going into the military, I needed to keep a sharp eye on the bottom line.

"No problem." Harry waved away the question of my hourly wage with a careless air that I envied. For me, any mention of money was quickly followed by a painful clutch in the gut. "How about you come over after school on Monday?" he said. "In fact, I'd better book you on a daily basis, huh? The way I'm going I'm facing an F. No joke—I'm desperate."

"I can't come Tuesday. That's my night at the parapsychology lab."

"You work at the parapsychology lab?"

"Yeah, I answer the phone on the nights the regular secretary is off."

"Funny thing—my dad does some consulting work out there."

"They use magicians? This is a joke, right?"

"Nah. Check it out. My dad will be listed on the yearly budget under 'sleight-of-hand consultants.' " He grinned. "Seriously, magicians are onto a lot of the tricks that these fake psychics use and the idea's to separate the real ones from fakes."

"I hadn't thought about that."

"Yeah, scientists are mostly pathetically trusting. You'd be surprised—they overlook really obvious stuff. Magicians are more suspicious. Houdini practically made a career out of unmasking psychics."

"I've heard of him. Wasn't he supposed to be the greatest magician ever or something?"

Harry smiled. "I don't know about that. I happen to think my dad and his partner are pretty good. Then there's David Copperfield. He's no slouch. Did you see the show when he made the Empire State Building disappear?"

"How did he do that?"

He shrugged. "Search me."

"So, are you thinking you'll follow in your dad's footsteps?"

"I say no—but who can tell? I'm no future rocket scientist, that's for sure. I can't even do algebra. So are we set up for tutoring on Monday? For sure?"

"Absolutely."

"Right after school, then?"

"Yup. I'm getting kind of curious about that mysterious mansion you live in."

"It's not very mysterious. Just a big, big old house. You watch, lady." The crooked grin again. "I'm going to monopolize your every waking moment between algebra and—other things."

The warm intimacy of his tone made me blush, which bothered me a lot. I think of myself as strictly a nonblushing type.

"Blythe!" Elizabeth's voice screeched in my ear, making me levitate a good two inches off my seat.

"Oh, hi, Elizabeth." I regarded her dubiously.

"I yelled to you coming out of the movie but you didn't even turn around. You must have had your mind on something else." She simpered at Harry. "Hey, aren't we in the same algebra class?"

"That's right," said Harry. "I'm the guy that sinks the curve."

"We can't all be math geniuses like Blythe," said Elizabeth sympathetically.

I regarded Elizabeth's remark about my being a math genius as a transparent attempt to ingratiate herself with Harry. She was wearing an earth-colored tunic and dangling earrings made up of coins. She had so many coins dripping from her ears she looked as if she were wearing her dowry. Her face was thin, her eyes were narrow, and I honestly could not think of her as competition. That's why when she hooked one of my onion rings, I managed to smile cordially.

"It's so hard to imagine Blythe being with anybody besides Quentin," said Elizabeth, sinking her teeth into the onion ring. "They've been a couple practically since kindergarten and when I look over here and see Blythe I keep expecting to see Quentin, too."

My smile grew fixed. "Come off it, Elizabeth."

"Seriously, it just seems so *weird.* Nothing against you or anything, Harry. It's just that it seems so unnatural. It's a shock to see you sitting with Blythe."

"It's more of a shock to Quentin, though, isn't it?" said Harry.

She lowered her voice, her face registering hokey compassion. "Honestly, he looks like death warmed over. He just can't believe it's happened."

"Well, that's enough about my love life, folks," I said brightly. "Don't you have a table of your own to go to, Elizabeth?"

"I'm going! I'm going. Do you want all the rest of those onion rings?"

"Yes!"

"Are you sure? They're fattening."

I must have been getting pink in the face because she backed away hastily, adding, "You really ought to work on that temper of yours. People with short fuses die young."

"If you don't go away it's going to be somebody else who dies young," I muttered.

"I'll see you in algebra, Harry," she trilled, wiggling her fingers in a wave.

"Elizabeth is a well-known eccentric," I said, once she was out of earshot.

"I figured there had to be some kind of logical explanation. Don't let her get to you."

"Do I look pink in the face?" When I patted my cheeks, they felt hot.

He considered me thoughtfully. "More like fuchsia."

"You'd think Quentin and I were joined at the hip the way some people are carrying on," I said. "I should have broken up with him a long time ago."

"It's nice to hear you say that. Everybody's been

telling me how you two were soulmates and the cutest couple, and all that stuff. I was beginning to wonder if I would ever get anywhere with you."

"You can try."

He gave me the kind of look that heats the surrounding atmosphere and took my hand. I explained very earnestly why I couldn't stand Elizabeth. He understood. I told him how my first grade teacher embarrassed me on the first day of school. He sympathized. I told him the entire story of my life. My onion rings got cold, and I didn't care. Everything seemed great as long as we were holding hands.

It was only later, when I got home, that I realized I still didn't know much about Harry.

Chapter 6

Dad left for Seymour Johnson Air Force Base early Monday morning. He planted a tearful good-bye kiss on my forehead and promised to come home and visit as soon as he could get leave. We both knew he wasn't going to get leave anytime soon since his unit was due to be shipped off any minute. As soon as he got in the car I had a premonition that he was going to step on a land mine. I was overcome with a terrible guilty feeling that I hadn't been very nice to him lately.

He took my car because he obviously wasn't going to be doing much driving. He left his for me to use. Watching him tool out of the subdivision in my car, the engine making odd, rattling noises, I felt very alone. I kept telling myself that I already paid the bills, carried out the garbage, and did the grocery shopping. So what did it matter that he was leaving? But when I went back in the house, it felt so empty I had to turn on the morning news to break the dead quiet. The voice of the announcer filled me in on local fires and burglaries while I got my things together for school.

I was relieved when I finally did get to school. The rattle of locker doors, the buzz of chatter, and the lukewarm water in the hall cooler all spelled "normal life" to me. Except conversation died every time I came up to any group. A few people looked at me funny. Obviously, everybody was talking about Quentin and me breaking up. From the way people were taking it, you'd think Barbie and Ken had announced their split.

I saw Quentin in the cafeteria at lunch. He was talking to Mandy Jenkins and I felt a white-hot stab of jealousy that frightened me. What was worse, he didn't seem to notice me.

All I have to do is crook my finger and I could have him back in a minute, I told myself. But I wasn't so sure of that anymore.

After school, Harry was standing by my car. "You're driving your dad's car now?" He gave it a curious glance.

"Yeah, he's already left for the base. He took mine."

He raised his eyebrows. "You mean you're all alone in the house?"

"You don't have to make a public announcement," I said. "Burglars might be listening." The morning news had had its effect on me.

"Oops! Sorry. Are we still on for tutoring this afternoon?"

"Sure. Why not?"

"I just thought I'd better warn you that it's a little complicated to get up to the house. You have to stop at the gate and ring the buzzer. Then I'll flip the switch to let you in."

"Have you always lived in a high-security prison?"

"It's just because of the animals," he said apologetically. "You don't have to worry about them. They've got their own part of the place and I'll lock them up before you come. We fenced the whole yard, though, because most of the time we give them the run of it. They like to swim in the pool."

I glanced up at him uneasily. "Uh, what kind of animals are we talking about here?"

"Pixie and Snowball." He grinned. "The tigers."

"You're making this up, aren't you?"

"Come and see for yourself."

I drove home and fortified myself with cookies and milk. May this house be safe from tigers, I thought. I wondered where I had heard that. It certainly seemed pertinent.

My mind was flooded with thoughts of Quentin. I wasn't sure what I felt anymore. I remembered pulling off the petals of flowers one by one—he loves me, he loves me not, as if the flower held the secret to someone else's mind. Silly. I couldn't even understand what was going on in my own mind. If I wanted to be rid of Quentin, why did I think about him so much?"

I rinsed out my glass, brushed the crumbs off the kitchen table, then got in Dad's car and drove to the Croger mansion. It was nothing if not convenient to my house. In no more than a few minutes I was turning into its entrance road. The road was lined on either side with trees and bordered by the tall fence. Soon I reached the gate and had to stop the car. I got out and looked up at the tall iron gate before me, not quite sure what to do next. The overhanging trees cast the gate into gloom. A dull metal box was fixed to a post at the left of it, and next to it was a neat plastic plate with white letters, "Tradesmen and guests ring bell please and speak into speaker."

I pressed the button, hoping it was working. I didn't hear any sound when I pressed it. At last a crack of static came from a speaker in the box. "Hello?" I said.

"Blythe? Is that you?" It was Harry's voice, but it sounded as if it were coming over the radio. "Get in the car and come on in," he said. "I'll open the gate."

When I got back in my car, the gate slowly slid to the side. Glancing in my rearview mirror as I drove on in, I saw it slide shut right behind my bumper, which gave me an odd feeling. The effect was unnervingly like a guillotine.

A long cement driveway led up to the gigantic brick house which was all of three stories tall with turrets, cupolas, and bay windows and lots of tall, skinny chimneys—the kind of place Dr. Jekyll and Mr. Hyde would have bedded down in. I almost expected to see a ghost come drifting out of one of its many chimneys. But unlike your typical haunted house the building had been very well kept. The brick had been recently repointed and the glossy black enamel of the front door and the brass door knocker gleamed in the sunlight. As I drove up to the house, a garage door slowly opened. Evidently I was expected to drive right in, instead of parking out front. In my opinion Harry's dad had gotten a little carried away with fancy electric-eye devices, but I suppose it was all worked out to keep guests from running into the tigers. By now I was more than ready to see an actual human being. I pulled into the dark garage, drawing my car up next to Harry's. A white Volvo was parked on the other side of it. The garage door closed shut behind me and a light came on. The cavernous garage was only dimly lit, but over in one corner I spotted the spangled spiral steps Harry had used in his act and standing next to them was a sturdy plywood staircase of the same height. I saw now how Harry had managed to vanish into thin air. Under cover of smoke, he had simply stepped through the stage curtains and stepped onto the plain plywood staircase that had been hidden there. Quentin was right, I thought. It was easy when you understood how it was done.

My eye caught a glimpse of what looked like a body wedged in the rafters and I recoiled, but a closer look revealed it was a department store dummy. Fancy papier-mâché hoops in bright colors were hung on the wall where most people would have put a lawnmower and clippers. Painted wooden cabinets lined the back wall. The garage was obviously where Harry's dad kept the bulky props used in his magic act.

A door to my left opened and a tall figure stood silhouetted darkly in it. Squinting, I made out that it was a tall blond man with hair cut so short as to look shaved. He was wearing a blue sweater over old jeans. When I had wished for a human being, I had pictured a more reassuring type.

I got out of the car. "I'm Blythe, Harry's algebra tutor?"

The man folded his arms over his muscular chest and regarded me warily for a moment before speaking. "Come in," he said at last. "You can wait inside."

He had a foreign accent I couldn't quite place—German, maybe?—and a face like a Viking marauder with beaked nose, blue eyes, and well-trimmed blond beard. His face was completely expressionless. Reluctantly, I followed him inside. I was beginning to have the creepy feeling Harry was playing a joke on me. Maybe he didn't live in this mansion after all. Maybe this man was a psychopathic creep who was luring me to my doom. But then I reminded myself that I had just seen Harry's car in the garage with a school parking sticker on it.

I followed the man into a large foyer with a marble floor. From there a sweeping iron and marble staircase curved up to the second story. Tall, thin windows with diamond-shaped panes were on either side of the front door, which didn't exactly let in floods of light. A huge chandelier overhanging the foyer was wired with lots of tiny electric lights, so the marble gleamed dully underneath it. "You can wait upstairs in the study," said the Viking.

I wanted to say, "No, thank you. I'll wait down here by the door in case I need to escape." But instead I meekly followed him up the stairs.

I remembered a stupid old monster movie I saw once where the heroine followed a fellow with a clumsily stitched-together face into a dark castle. I always thought it wasn't very realistic for the girl to go along with the monster but all of a sudden I understood her motivation. She was afraid of looking foolish. The fear of looking foolish was a surprisingly powerful force. It was certainly all that kept me climbing up that staircase.

The sound of my footsteps died when I stepped onto the Oriental rug at the top of the stairs. I noticed that my fingers, gripping the banister tightly, were faintly blue. I glanced out over the stairwell and saw that the windows over the stairs were of stained glass, mostly red and blue, with only touches of other colors. The windows depicted some medieval maiden getting the worst of it in an encounter with a dragon. Light streaming through the glass threw patches of colored light onto the banisters, which accounted for my blue fingers. The colored light that came in through the windows did little to dispel the gloom. In my opinion, the place could have done with a few gallons of white paint and some nice posters to cheer it up.

"You can wait there," said the Viking. He pointed toward the open door to a dimly lit room lined with tall bookcases.

As soon as I stepped in, the door closed behind me, which made me jump a little. The marble tiles on the floor were arranged in alternating black and white squares like a chessboard. I had the unnerving feeling for a second that I was a pawn on the chessboard, but I did my best to remain calm. I looked around me. This room would be a good place to do algebra tutoring, I told myself. It was quiet—no distractions. In fact, it was almost too quiet, I thought nervously. As if it had been soundproofed. The stuffed polar bear head which hung over the mantel had red glass eyes and the chairs, including the one at the desk, were covered in red plush to match. This was, in my opinion, questionable taste, but then Harry had warned me that his dad's place was a bit over the top. Grandeur as interpreted by the Addams family, perhaps? The fireplace must have been just for burning incriminating documents because old-fashioned radiators stood under the windows. I sat down, the red plush of the chair tickling my legs, and prepared to wait. How long could it take to fetch Harry, after all? I glanced at my watch.

My resolve to remain calm didn't last long. In less than two minutes I was up, pacing tight arcs on the checkerboard floor. I peered anxiously out the window and saw it was barred outside with ornate iron bars. From the height of the second story I could see the blue rectangle of a swimming pool and what looked like striped cabanas on a broad terrace below. A movement caught my attention at the edge of my range of vision but before I could even turn my head for a better look, there was a flash of movement and a splash in the pool. I saw an animal's head surface and then move slowly, followed by the shiny vee of its wake as it swam through the water. The beast's head, large and damply shaggy, had a blunt feline snout. I wished I had binoculars to get a closer look, but I knew it was one of the tigers. Suddenly, I couldn't wait for Harry any longer. I strode to the door and twisted the knob, but it wouldn't turn. Scarcely able to believe it, I twisted it again. I wrenched at it until my hand hurt, but the knob wouldn't move. When I bent to peer at the crack between the door and the doorjamb, I saw that the bolt was shot into place. I kicked the door. "Harry!" I shrieked. Silence. I ran to the window and threw it open only to see the ornate iron bars. I was trapped! Suddenly I realized that no one even knew where I was. My father had driven off for the air force base this morning and was probably still on the road. How long would it take for him to become alarmed at getting no answer from the phone at home? Even if he eventually called the police, they wouldn't know where to look for me. I hadn't told anyone where I was going.

"This can't be happening," I said aloud. "This is some kind of mistake." But the sound of my voice in the empty room only made me feel more panicky.

I threw open the desk drawers and hastily rifled the papers in them. Perhaps I could find a key. The desk was full of letters and papers, paper clips, pencils, erasers. But no key. A letter opener winked among the paper clips and I snatched it up. Brass and pointed like a knife, it was the closest thing I had to a weapon. I opened the window and pried at the edges of the iron bars. But instead of being fixed to the outside, they had been sandwiched between the rows of brick. I knew I would never dislodge them. I was careful to keep a firm grip on the letter opener. I didn't want it to slip out of my grasp and go skittering down the roof.

Convinced there was no way to get out the window, I turned around and stared at the fireplace. Chimney sweeps went up fireplaces, didn't they? Maybe I could, too. I knelt on the hearth and peered upward. nothing but perfect blackness. Either the chimney did not go directly up or else a flue or damper was blocking my way. No escape. My knees and hands were smeared with ashes and there were flecks of ashes on my skirt. I stood up, pulled a tissue out of my pocket, and began scrubbing at my knees.

Just then the door opened.

"Cinderella?" asked Harry, his mouth twisted in a quizzical smile. "Don't tell me, let me guess. You were trying to start a fire."

"Very funny," I said hotly. "If this is your idea of a joke, I don't think much of it. You can walk me to my car, now, thank you."

"Hey, you aren't really mad, are you?" He looked crestfallen.

"Oh, no! I'm perfectly accustomed to being locked up in strange houses." I pushed my hair out of my eyes, uncomfortably conscious that I must be leaving a trail of ash across my face.

"I'm sorry about this. Karl is just skittish. He didn't know you were coming to tutor. He thought you might be some kind of spy."

I looked at him blankly. "Spy? What kind of spy could I possible be?"

"For some other act. You could be trying to get at our trade secrets," he said. "Dad and Karl are always watching out for the competition. The magician business is really cutthroat."

"You're saying your friend Karl took me for a rival magician? That's the most ridiculous thing I've ever heard! The algebra book was just part of my clever disguise, I suppose!"

"Go ahead and laugh, but the number-one spy business in the country these days is people after trade secrets. Truth! Hey, why don't we go downstairs and get you something to drink?" He lifted his eyebrows questioningly. "Are we friends?"

"Why don't I just go downstairs and *leave?*" I snatched up my purse and my algebra book and stormed out of the room.

He followed right behind me. "You aren't going to make me do my homework all by myself, are you? I don't understand the first thing about it. Honestly! I'm desperate."

"You should have thought about that before you let your dad's gorilla lock me up in that room." I made my way down the stairs.

"It was just a mix-up," he said plaintively. "I've been looking all over for you. I forgot to lock up Pixie and Snowball before you came and I was afraid maybe you'd gotten out of your car and gone outside."

"That would have been just too bad, wouldn't it? I guess I would have been eaten by the tigers, then. That *would* have been a merry mix-up."

"Oh, I don't think they'd hurt you," he said. "I was just afraid you might get spooked if you ran into them by accident. But it only took me a few minutes to figure out that you must have gone inside. Then I ran into Karl and he told me where you were. Won't you at least sit down a minute before you go?"

I could feel myself weakening. Maybe I had overreacted. I reminded myself that I could definitely use the five dollars an hour I would get for the tutoring. "Oh, all right," I said crossly. "I guess I'll stay."

Harry hung a key on a key rack by the door. I noticed that it had a charm hanging from it. Harry followed my gaze. "I guess you noticed everything's run by radio signals," he said. "Dad loves that kind of thing. But the first thunderstorm, the whole system went down. It was crazy—the gates opened and closed and then they wouldn't open at all. The tigers were roaring, totally freaked out, and we weren't all that calm either. After that we got a locksmith out here to put in a backup system. Everything opens with a simple house key." He took it down and showed it to me. A shiny tiger-shaped charm dangled from it. "Sometimes the simple way is best." He smiled and hung the key back in its place.

I noticed that the kitchen, unlike the rest of the house, was plain and modern. Refrigerator magnets in the shape of daisies held illegibly scrawled notes onto the refrigerator door. An assortment of potted plants stood in front of a big bay window that had a view of the patio and the swimming pool beyond it. It was a perfectly ordinary kitchen. But as I watched, the illusion of normality was shattered when a huge, wet tiger padded silently across the patio outside, the fur at its jowls standing out in untidy dripping points. It left large, damp paw prints behind it on the stone.

"Here, kitty, kitty," I said weakly. It was my feeble attempt at a joke, but when the tiger swung its huge head slowly around and looked straight at me through the glass windows, my blood froze.

"Gorgeous, isn't he?" asked Harry. Behind me, the soft drink fizzed on ice.

"Very," I said, backing off from the window. I wondered if tigers ever took flying leaps through glass.

"He's a snow tiger. That's why he's black and white instead of butter-colored. Dad hand-raised both of ours. They're great for the act. A rabbit is one thing, but when a tiger leaps through a paper hoop it knocks the audience out. Seriously. No other magic act has anything remotely like it."

"I guess not." I sank into a kitchen chair. "Do you have any other pets?" I glanced under the table, fearful that boa constrictors or worse might be lurking in this odd household.

"Well, we've got the rabbits," said Harry. "We used to give them the run of the house, but they bit right through electrical cords and before we knew it none of the appliances were working. So now we keep them in cages on the third floor. For a while we had them in hutches outside, which made it easier to clean up after them, but Snowball and Pixie kept jumping at them and we lost quite a few bunnies that way."

"The tigers ate them?" I cried, startled.

"No, Snowball and Pixie were just playing, but the rabbits kept keeling over from heart attacks. They're better off inside."

"Maybe there's a reason why people stick with dogs and cats. I guess next you're going to tell me that Snowball and Pixie are vegetarians."

"No, we feed them sides of beef plus a food supplement." He pushed the foaming glass of soft drink toward me and opened his algebra book. "I've already started on problem one." He shot a pleading look at me. "Couldn't you help me out? I'm getting nowhere."

Every household has its little oddities, I told myself. The tigers, the barred windows, and the locked doors were, considered in one way, just a part of Harry's dad's business, no more exotic than used cars would be to a used-car salesman, or pigs to a pig farmer.

Quentin had never needed my help at schoolwork. Unlike Harry, Quentin always set the curve. It was rather pleasant to be needed. I pulled my chair over next to Harry's and glanced at his paper. "To start with, let's try writing the problems out legibly," I suggested.

"When I look at the page I get sick to my stomach and go all to pieces."

"You just need to get organized."

"That isn't all I need," he said woefully. He lay his hand over mine and looked at me. "I need help," he said.

I felt a little tremor of something that might have been attraction. If I could get past the little quirks in Harry's household, it was very possible we might have a rewarding relationship, and, after all, the five dollars an hour, I reminded myself, was definitely a plus.

Chapter 7

Tuesday night Dad called from the base. "I had to wait in line forever to get to the phone," he said. "The last guy must have talked twenty minutes. How's it going?"

I was careful not to tell him about my adventure over at Harry's. It would only worry him. "Everything's fine here." I glanced at my watch. I was already running late for my job.

"Rumors are flying around all over the place here. I can't figure out if we're going to be shipped off tomorrow or next month. Everything's hush-hush. Maybe they'll keep us three days and let us go home," he said hopefully.

Ever the optimist, my dad. "Are you taking your vitamins? Are you getting enough sleep?" I asked.

"I'm fine," he said with false heartiness. "You just take care of yourself and don't worry about me."

It was ten after seven when we finished talking, but I figured my boss would understand, so I wasn't too worried. What was particularly nice was that I had Dad's car to drive to the lab. It was a monstrously big vehicle from the seventies and its vinyl roof needed three hundred dollars worth of repairs, which it obviously was not going to get. Also it left a permanent black stain under it because it had an oil leak, but it seemed new compared to my ancient heap. Equally important, its lights weren't shorting out. I wasn't up to any more unnerving incidents on the road.

I allowed myself to speed a little on the way. The road out to the lab had once been busy, our town's main route to Durham and its international airport almost two hours away through a handful of small towns. But then the bypass had been built out north of the Croger mansion when I was in grade school. The new route shaved almost a half hour off the driving time to Durham, so the traffic had moved to the bypass. These days the road to the lab was mostly used by the few local people who lived out this way and tractors making their way to farm fields. I knew it didn't get many patrolling police cars. Or road repair crews, for that matter.

As soon as I got to the lab I rushed inside, shucking my jacket as I went in. In my hurry I nearly collided with a man standing just inside the door.

"Here she is," said Dr. Burrows. "This is Blythe. She fills in for our receptionist."

The slender, blond man eyed me curiously. "Oh, I know Blythe. Or at least I know of her. She's tutoring my son in algebra."

I smiled uncertainly as I made my way to my desk. I could see a resemblance between this man and Harry, if I looked for it. They were both fair. They had the same long mouth and the same build. But this man had a pronouncedly broad forehead and a map of creases around the eyes when he smiled. He smiled in a friendly way as he put on his leather gloves.

"Jack is our fraud detector," said Dr. Burrows.

"I like to think of myself as a sleight-of-hand consultant," Mr. Weaver said with a smile.

"Jack is a magician of some note. We're lucky to have him."

"Oh, I take a real interest in the work," said Mr. Weaver mildly. "Nice meeting you, Blythe. I guess I'll be seeing you." He nodded, then slipped out the door in an understated way that seemed to be a family trait.

"I've been answering the phone, since you were running late," said Dr. Burrows. "I hope I haven't made a hash of the messages. I jotted some down there on the blotter."

"The reason I'm late is that m-my father called from the base," I stuttered. "He's not sure when he's going to be shipped out."

"No problem. Don't worry about it. I knew there had to be a good reason." Dr. Burrows leafed through some papers. "Some of the people who call here really sound like nuts, don't they? I never realized."

We exchanged smiles. Just then I heard a roar outside the door that was so loud it sounded like the universe unzipping.

"What's that?" I cried.

Dr. Burrows didn't even turn around. "That's Jack Weaver's motorcycle. You couldn't get me on one of those things. They're death traps."

He disappeared into his office still shuffling papers. I stood frozen at my desk for a moment, unable to move. Harry's dad rode a motorcycle? I remembered the biker who had followed me home. Could he be—

I sat down in my swivel chair. The idea was ridiculous. Just because Harry's dad was a magician, I was letting my imagination run away with me. Jack

Weaver was a perfectly respectable businessman who just happened to be in a rather offbeat business.

"No different from a pig farmer," I said aloud.

Dr. Burrows opened his office door. "Did you say something, Blythe?" He shot me a puzzled look.

I blushed hotly. "No, sir."

The next day at school, Quentin cornered me at my locker. "What's going on, Blythe? I kept calling you last night and you weren't home."

"It's my night to work at the parapsychology lab, remember?" I was so pleased to see him I was afraid it showed.

"Oh. Of course, I remember. It's just that I don't know if I'm coming or going these days. Where were you Monday afternoon? I tried you again and again before play practice."

"I was tutoring," I said. "Look, I don't owe you any explanations, Quentin. We aren't going together anymore."

"It wouldn't happen to be Harry you're tutoring, would it?"

"So what if it is?" I pulled my books out of my locker and my notebooks spilled on the floor in my confusion.

"That tutoring's just a scheme so he can take up every minute of your time. I'm surprised you didn't see through that."

"Quentin, I'm not going to talk to you about Harry. It's stupid."

Suddenly Harry was standing beside me and I jumped. It was unnerving the way he appeared out of nowhere. As he gazed at Quentin a slow smile spread over his face. "Hi," he said.

Quentin's eyes narrowed. "So, I hear you and your dad have fixed up the old Croger mansion."

I glanced at Harry anxiously, but he only seemed amused. "Yeah, we got big plans. Why are you so interested in where I live all of a sudden, huh?"

"Naturally, I worry about who Blythe's hanging out with. When it turns out nobody knows anything about you and your weird old mansion except you've put up the biggest fence anybody's ever seen around here I ask myself what you're hiding."

"The fence is there because—" I began.

Harry interrupted. "We don't have to explain anything to him, Blythe. Not a thing."

"I don't get it," said Quentin. "Why are you all of a sudden after Blythe?" His eyes narrowed, as if he truly could not understand Harry's being attracted to me.

I bristled, offended in spite of myself at his attitude. Harry was right—I didn't owe Quentin any explanations.

Harry pulled me toward him and stroked my hair. "I like Blythe."

Quentin flushed. "I don't know what's going on here, but I can see you're just trying to get at me. Okay, you've gotten at me. There's no point in me acting like I don't care. I do."

I was touched in spite of myself that he was standing right there by my locker, a place as public as a stadium, and admitting that he was hurt. I noticed the way his hair curled damply at his temple and wanted to hug him, but it was impossible. Harry had his arms around me and was nuzzling my ear. I had no idea my life could get so complicated.

Quentin reddened, turned around abruptly, and disappeared into the curious crowd.

I pushed Harry away. "Quentin's right, isn't he? You were just trying to get to him. It isn't very nice of you."

"I'm not a very nice person." He smiled at me.

"Gee, for a minute there, I thought we were going to have a fight," a sophomore exclaimed in disappointment.

"What's Quentin's problem?" said Harry. "He's pretty dumb if he thinks making a scene is the way to get you back."

The bell for homeroom rang and I had to run to get to class. I was breathless when I slid into my desk. I could feel myself melting toward Quentin. So he wasn't as cool and controlled as Harry—I liked him the better for it. He cared enough about me to make a fool out of himself right in front of everybody. It was sweet. I found myself remembering that we had been good together once.

Marcy Wilder leaned toward me. "Did you hear what happened? That girl in the car accident with Quentin killed herself."

"No!" I cried.

"Yeah, my cousin went to school with her and she told me. She tried to kill herself a couple of times after the accident and finally she did it. Isn't it awful?"

"How—how did she do it?"

Marcy shook her head. "I don't know the details. My cousin said it was in the paper, but I didn't see it, did you? It's so sad."

Unconsciously my hand touched my face and the coldness of my fingers seemed to bring me to. "Awful," I breathed. All the reasons I'd broken up with Quentin came back to me, and I realized I could never get back together with him now.

At lunchtime, my one thought was to find some

quiet place to sort out my feelings. I wasn't a bit hungry and just at the moment I didn't want to see either Harry or Quentin, but when I dipped into the library I ran smack into Elizabeth. "I heard all about Quentin socking Harry," she said with relish.

"Quentin didn't sock Harry," I replied automatically.

"Rick Sumner saw it. He thought maybe Harry said something to Quentin but all of a sudden Quentin hauled off and socked him."

"Elizabeth, you know very well Quentin has never been in a fight in his life."

"There's always a first time," she trilled happily. "Besides, it wasn't really a fight because Biff pulled Quentin off and got him out of there. You know what this means. Quentin's going to get suspended."

"I've got to go eat lunch," I said, turning on my heel. I had to get away from that gloating face. Why did I even bother to be polite to her?

When I finally did go into the cafeteria, I had the feeling everyone was staring at me. As I got in the lunch line, my cheeks burned. I felt a warm hand at my waist and wheeled around in alarm but it was only Harry. He had a Band-Aid on his chin. "Oh, no," I cried. "Is that where he hit you?"

Harry fingered the Band-Aid. "No big deal."

"Does it hurt?"

He frowned. "It's no big deal, Blythe. Drop it, will you?"

It occurred to me that he was a little embarrassed that he hadn't hit back. Of course, the idea was absurd. He was half a head shorter than Quentin and besides, it sounded as if Biff had pulled Quentin away too fast for anything else to happen. "I hope we're not having meat loaf again," I said.

He grinned. "Nice try, Blythe. I hope it's not meat loaf, too. God knows what they put in the stuff. Probably ground-up horses. We'll all start to neigh next."

It was meat loaf and while we ate it we talked about the upcoming algebra test, the possible things that could have been ground up in the meat loaf, and the tigers. Anything but what was really on our minds—Quentin.

"I used to play this game of hiding from the tigers in the tall grass," Harry chortled. "Mom flipped out when she came outside and realized Snowball and Pixie were stalking us."

"I can't imagine why."

"She said we couldn't play with the tigers anymore." The smile faded from his lips. "It wasn't too long after that that my parents split."

"Over the tigers?"

"Nah, Mom liked Snowball and Pixie. Heck, she used to feed them their bottles all the time. She was just afraid they'd get carried away and pounce on us so hard they'd break our backs. I guess it was dangerous. The tigers grew up without us exactly noticing it."

"Who's 'us'? I thought you were an only child."

"Yeah. I am." His face closed down and I knew the subject of his childhood was closed. I had noticed before that Harry didn't like to talk about himself. It was certainly a change from Quentin who could go on with funny stories about his second grade teacher or complaints about his swim coach for hours.

Harry stood up and picked up his tray.

"So, are you and I on for tutoring this afternoon?" I asked to break the silence.

"Isn't this your day for the parapsychology lab?"

I blinked, surprised I had forgotten. “Oh. Well, see you tomorrow, then.”

“Sure.” His face was blank.

I stared after him, wondering what on earth I had said wrong.

Chapter 8

The next morning, I darted nervous glances up and down the hall. No sign of Quentin. I realized that I was hoping he would come breezing by my locker the way he so often did in the morning. Except for the absence of Quentin, everything was the same. Michael and Amy were making out over by the stairs. Julie King bounded out of the girls' room, reeking of smoke, and threw a friendly smile in my direction. I started after her, thinking I would ask if she had seen Quentin, but with her long legs she quickly outdistanced me and disappeared into the crowd. I was feeling lost when I suddenly collided with Elizabeth.

We both stooped to pick up our spilled books as the traffic surged around us. "Have you seen Quentin?" Elizabeth asked. "I was supposed to give him the minutes of the Student Council meeting this morning before class, but I can't find him anywhere."

Suddenly I realized what must have happened. "He must have been suspended!" I exclaimed.

"He wasn't suspended!"

"He must have been! For hitting Harry yesterday. For a minute there, it slipped my mind."

"Well, you can forget it," said Elizabeth flatly. "Nobody told on him. You can take it from me that nobody breathed a word. Some smart-aleck sophomore wanted to turn informer but Biff let him know that none of us would appreciate it."

"But if he didn't get suspended, then where is he?" I asked. It never even occurred to me that he might be sick. Quentin never was sick.

"We must have missed him somehow," said Elizabeth, looking around.

I went on to homeroom, but I was uneasy. Without quite being able to put the thought into words, I realized it was hard to miss Quentin. He commanded the hallways with the sure touch of one who was born to be a star. He was never inconspicuous.

At lunchtime I couldn't find Harry, and I had to fight the insane feeling that he and Quentin were off somewhere fighting. I spotted Elizabeth and sat down beside her. "Did you ever find Quentin?"

She shook her head. "He's not here today. I asked Mandy Frame—she's in his homeroom—and she said he was absent. Do you think he's run away from home? He was pretty upset after that fight with Harry yesterday."

"That's ridiculous. Why would he run away?"

"Just an idea."

I quelled the impulse to tell her to get a life. Harry laid a hand on my shoulder. "We're still on for tutoring this afternoon, aren't we?" he said.

I glanced up at him, conscious that he was breathing more quickly than usual. "I guess. Where have you been? Have you already had lunch?"

"I'm not hungry. I'll see you at the usual time, then. I gotta go. See you."

He was gone before I could say anything.

"You two seem to be very close," said Elizabeth sarcastically. "Do you tutor him often?"

"I think I'm going to. Harry has quite a struggle with algebra."

Elizabeth slurped her milk noisily. "He must. We don't even have any homework this week. Mrs. Haley is out for gallbladder surgery and we have a substitute all week."

"Elizabeth, why don't you call up Quentin and find out if he's sick?" I suggested.

"Why don't you call him up yourself?"

"I can't do that!"

"I tell you what I think. I think you aren't as fed up with Quentin as you like to pretend. What would you say if I said you're just as emotional about this breakup as Quentin is and that you're just kidding yourself thinking you two can stay apart? Huh? What would you say to that?"

"Good-bye, Elizabeth," I said. I stood up, grabbed my tray, and fled. Where did she get off telling me what I was feeling? Steam was coming out my ears all the way back to class.

The rest of the day I was careful not to ask if anybody had heard anything about Quentin. Not even when I saw Biff in the parking lot after school. The last thing I wanted people to think was that I was pining away for Quentin. We were through. Absolutely finished. It was just that I felt slightly uneasy when I didn't see him in the morning as usual.

After school, following an impulse I scarcely understood, I drove over to the Woodcroft neighborhood, to Holly Street where Quentin lived. As I got closer to the house, I began to get nervous that he would look out the window and recognize the car. I didn't want him to think I couldn't stop myself from driving by his house—that would be too pathetic. Glancing down the row of neatly manicured lawns, I was startled to see a police car parked in front of Quentin's house, not a patrol car with a blue light on the top, but an administrative-type car with the simple logo of the city police department on the door. I had the sudden crazy conviction that Quentin's parents were filing a missing person report.

Slowly, letting the car run on idle, I inched by Quentin's house. Its blank face gave nothing away. I could make out the pale outlines of the swagged draperies in the living room, but light glanced off the windows so that they might as well have been opaque for all I could see inside.

Panic swept over me. What had happened to Quentin? Suddenly I missed him almost more than I could bear. I wanted to run up to his front door and bang on it, but I was afraid of what I would find out.

Swiftly, I pulled away. I couldn't go home to my empty house. My heart was thumping painfully. Calm down, I kept telling myself futilely. It's probably nothing. Nothing at all. But when I caught a glimpse of myself in the rearview mirror, my eyes were wild and my face was pale, as if I had seen something terrible. I drove on past the Holmhaven subdivision sign and turned in at the entry road to the Croger mansion. This time I scarcely noticed the big trees that overhung the gate of the mansion and cast it into gloom. I was impervious to atmosphere. All I could think about was the police car in front of Quentin's house.

I got out and pressed the buzzer. Harry's disembodied voice came at me.

"Come on in," he said. "I'm opening the gate now. Drive slow, though. The tigers are out."

The last thing I wanted to do was meet up with a snow tiger. But as I drove up to the house, I didn't see any sign of the animals.

Harry stood at the open side door to the garage, waiting for me. I jumped out of the car, ignoring the gigantic papier-mâché daisy that hung over my car next to the bare body of a manikin.

I bounded up the few steps to the door, eager to escape the huge, gloomy garage. Harry caught me and flung his arms around me. "Whoa! What's all the excitement?"

"I just drove by Quentin's house and the cops were there!"

I felt him stop breathing for a moment. Then he pushed me away from him into the kitchen and regarded me with narrowed eyes. "So, what are you trying to tell me?"

I shook my head. "I don't know. I'm not even sure myself what it means. What do you think? Quentin wasn't at school today and when I drove by his house there was a police car there. Not a patrol car, exactly. More the kind of thing the police chief must drive."

"Want something to eat?" he asked absently.

I shook my head. "Do you think something could have happened to him?" I asked.

"What could have happened?" He got a liter-sized bottle of soda out of the fridge. "It's probably nothing." He looked at me curiously. "What were you doing driving by Quentin's house? Lonesome for him?"

I flushed. "I don't know. I was just over in that direction—"

"And the car knows the way?" he suggested gently. "It's okay, Blythe. You don't owe me any explanation." He pushed a bowl of potato chips in my direction.

"I don't know what it is," I said, "but I guess seeing that police car over there bothered me. What if

Quentin's been kidnapped? I know it sounds silly." I shrugged self-consciously. "I guess I'm imagining things. Since Dad left I'm kind of on edge."

"Yeah, I keep forgetting. You're all alone in the house now."

"I wish you wouldn't say it that way," I said, irritated. "You sound like you expect a walking mummy to pay me a visit just because my dad's out of town."

Harry dumped the potato chips back in the bag and closed it with a plastic clip. He had the slightly blank look on his face of a person who's listening to a distant channel on earphones. "Tell you what," he said. "Why don't we do something a little different before we start work. Do you want to meet Snowball and Pixie?"

"The tigers?"

"Yeah. Remember, I told you they were outside."

Involuntarily, I glanced out the big bow window at the pool, but no shaggy head marred the smoothness of the blue surface of the water.

"Don't most people drain their pools in the winter?" I asked.

"We heat ours enough to keep it from freezing. Dad doesn't like to drain it because Pixie and Snowball love to swim."

"I don't see them now." I guess I was hoping he'd say in that case forget it and we'll get right down to working on algebra.

"No problem," he said. "I'll call them."

I hesitated. "I'm not sure—"

Harry laughed softly. "You aren't going to tell me you're afraid of them? I told you Dad hand-raised them. They think they're human."

The way he talked, I felt silly. How dangerous could the tigers be, I told myself, if Mr. Weaver used them in his act? After all, if they gobbled up members of the audience, it wasn't likely his act would get many bookings.

"All right," I agreed reluctantly.

Removing the tiger charm key ring from the rack, Harry opened the door by the bay window and we went out to the pool. A few leaves floated on the still water. He got a long-handled net from a locked shed and began raking the leaves off the surface of the water. I scanned the stretch of lawn surrounding the pool. Beyond the immediate cleared area was a bank of trees and overgrown woods myrtle bushes, and beyond that was the long fence that enclosed the property. The house was set far in from the main road and the property was thick with trees. I couldn't even hear the hum of passing trucks, an invariable and familiar sound from my own bedroom. It had the feel, almost, of being out in the middle of a vast, wooded wilderness except that beyond the fence was a gap in the trees. Some smaller road must run behind the property. The fence advanced to the east on my right until it was lost in the big trees. Perhaps the tigers' usual quarters were farther into the trees, I thought, out of sight.

"Are you going to call Snowball and Pixie?" I asked Harry. Not that I was in any hurry to meet them. My only worry was that they would come bounding at me unexpectedly. If they were going to show up I wanted to be ready.

"In a minute," said Harry. "I don't want these leaves to gunk up the filter. You can call them if you want."

"No thanks. I'll wait." I sat down on a cold metal chair and pulled my jacket tightly around me.

"They're around here somewhere," said Harry,

reaching for an elusive leaf. "You can stroll around and have a look while I finish this up."

It was then I noticed that the branches of one of the woods myrtles was moving. A low sound like a motor seemed to come from nowhere. I cleared my throat. "I think one of them must be over in the bushes," I said.

Harry turned around. "What's he into?" He dumped the leaves into a plastic garbage bin. "Go check on him, Blythe. I hope they aren't into something they aren't supposed to be into. Those bushes are where they go to hide things. They'd better not have somebody's pet cat."

What an awful thought! My pulse was racing as I reluctantly approached the woods myrtle bush. "Snowball?" I called in a faint voice. "Pixie?" The bush quit moving, as if the tiger had frozen at the sound of my voice, and the hair on the back of my neck stood on end. Without consciously planning to, I began backing away.

Harry dropped the rake with a clatter. "What are they up to?"

He strode past me, parting the bushes, leaves and twigs snapping noisily under his feet. He was only a few yards ahead of me when he suddenly froze. "Blythe," he said in a strange voice. "Go back to the house and call 911."

"What is it?" I cried. I pressed past him in a sudden panic. The woods myrtle bushes tugged at my hair. I saw a white hand lying on the leaves. A low growl came from the bushes and a slight movement revealed the shaggy head of the tiger bent on its task of gnawing on the bloodied blue sleeve of its victim. The tiger's snout was caked with blood. "Make him stop!" I screamed, grabbing at Harry's arm. "Stop him!"

"Snowball!" snapped Harry. "Back off!"

But the tiger only shook its prey and tried to back more deeply into the bushes. "It's a person!" I screamed. "The tiger's killed somebody! We've got to stop him."

Before I knew what I was doing, I plunged ahead into the bushes. A flurry of movement sent a spray of leaves in my face. Pushing them out of the way, I looked down suddenly and saw Quentin's face, his dead eyes open and staring at me. His face was smeared with blood and his usually neat hair was matted with it. Leaves and branches tore at me as I turned and stumbled away. I heard someone screaming steadily, hysterically, and realized with vague surprise that it was me.

Chapter 9

Harry dragged me away from Quentin and made me sit on the back steps. "Dad!" he yelled.

But Mr. Weaver had obviously already heard my screams. He burst out the back door at once.

"It's a guy from school," Harry said. "Out in the bushes. He's dead."

"I better get an ambulance," said Mr. Weaver, darting quickly back to the kitchen.

It seemed bizarre to send for an ambulance. I had never doubted, from the moment I saw Quentin's empty eyes, that he was dead. I sat on the back steps shivering and hugging my knees.

Harry went inside and got a blanket to wrap around me. "Put your head down," he urged me. "You're in shock."

"L-leave me alone." My teeth chattered. I was shaking all over and couldn't seem to stop.

At last the ambulance came. A police car pulled up beside the pool next to the ambulance. Two police officers got out and Mr. Weaver briefly explained to them what had happened. "It was a classmate of my son's," he explained. "For some reason he must have climbed over the fence." He shook his head. "We always keep the place locked tight because of the animals, so that's the only way he could have gotten in. What a crazy thing to do!"

I saw flashes of light in the shrubbery and realized someone was taking pictures. I felt dazed. It was as if this were happening to someone else. I seemed to be watching myself from a long way off. A few minutes later, the paramedics rolled a stretcher past the pool and pushed it into the tangled bushes. Minutes later, they rolled the stretcher out. A white linen sheet covered Quentin's body. One of the paramedics doubled over and retched into the bushes. A minute later they rolled the stretcher into the ambulance. I stared at it in disbelief. It seemed incredible that the long rise under the white drapery could be Quentin. I had an insane impulse to jump up and rip the sheet off as if doing that would prove he wasn't there. The greatest magic trick of all—I would whip away the white cloth and everything that had happened so far would turn out to be an illusion. But I knew it was real. The sign of Quentin's face, so familiar yet suddenly strangely slack and lifeless, was burned into my brain. I gripped my knees tightly and bit my lip so hard it bled.

The ambulance drove away.

"He must have fractured his skull in the fall," put in Harry. "I heard one of the paramedics say it looked like a fractured skull."

One of the police officers tipped his cap up with his pencil and regarded Jack Weaver seriously. "Now, your son discovered the body you say?"

"My son and Blythe here, who tutors him in algebra." Mr. Weaver glanced at me apologetically.

"We'll need to have statements from them."

"Yes, yes, of course," said Mr. Weaver. "But I

think Harry had better drive Blythe home right now. You can see yourself that she's in shock."

The other police officer knelt beside me. "We'll just need your name, address, and telephone number, miss, before you leave." He took down the relevant information. I was doing fine on the name and address, and I started to say I could go ahead and give him a statement now, but as soon as I began thinking of Quentin, hot tears spilled down my cheeks and I knew I was about to break down.

"Harry, why don't you drive Blythe home in your car," said Mr. Weaver hastily. "I can bring her car."

Harry and his father headed toward the house, the two police officers were back by the bushes talking in whispers, and I suddenly felt chilled to the bone and totally alone. The reality of what had happened was beginning to hit me. Dead. Quentin was dead. I would never see him again. The thought was like a shard of broken glass in my heart. Something was dreadfully wrong and couldn't be put right.

As I stumbled toward a lawn chair by the pool, a glittering object in the grass caught my eye. It was the tiger charm, dangling from the key Harry had taken from the rack by the door. He must have dropped it in the chaos after the discovery of Quentin's body. I reached for it and slipped it in my pocket, thinking absently that I had to give it to Harry.

Minutes later I was in the front seat of the big car next to Harry, my teeth still chattering. I was glad not to have to drive.

"I hope the police don't get all weird about the tigers," Harry said.

I giggled until I hiccupped.

"Cut it out, Blythe," said Harry sharply. "You're getting hysterical. Do you want me to pull over?"

I covered my mouth with my hand. A bit later, he pulled the car up into my driveway. Mr. Weaver followed in my car.

"Do you want me to come in with you?" he asked.

I shook my head.

"Are you sure you're going to be okay?"

"I'll be fine." My knees felt weak, but it was a point of pride for me to get into the house by myself and I believed I could pull it off. "Bye," I said. I slid out of the car.

"I'll call you later," said Harry.

"I may go to bed," I said. I walked to my front door. Once inside, I watched out the kitchen window until they drove away. Then I put my head down on the table and wept as though my heart would break.

The neighborhood was gray with twilight when Angela Wachtel's little Mazda pulled into the driveway. I hadn't thought to turn on the light inside, so her knock at the kitchen door was hesitant. She must have wondered if I was at home. Or since my car was obviously in the driveway maybe she was worried something awful had happened to me. She seemed relieved to see me when I opened the door. "Pack up your things," she said. "You're coming home with me. Mom agrees you ought not to be here by yourself after what happened."

I fell into a kitchen chair. "You heard what happened." My voice was hoarse.

"Elizabeth called me. Her mom and Quentin's mom are cousins. I just couldn't believe it at first. It seems too unreal." She brushed at her cheek with the back of her hand.

"I saw him," I said. "The tiger was chewing on him."

Angela jumped up suddenly and switched on the kitchen light. "Don't think about it, Blythe. It's just too awful." Then she turned on the light over the sink and the light over the kitchen stove, as if she were trying to banish another kind of darkness.

"What was he doing over at Harry's?" I asked. "Why would he go there?"

She regarded me anxiously. "I don't know."

"He wouldn't go over to Harry's and climb that big fence just because he was jealous of him," I insisted. "It doesn't make any sense!"

"Could—could he have been trying to play a trick on Harry?" she suggested hesitantly. "That's the kind of thing Quentin might try to do, isn't it? Some kind of stunt or practical joke, maybe?"

"But what?"

"I guess we'll never know."

I balled up my fist and hit the table. "I can't stand it," I cried.

"Just throw together some things and you can come home with me." Angela patted my shoulder gingerly. "My mom will take care of you."

I laughed a little. Unless her mom could bring Quentin back to life there was nothing she could do for me, but I knew she only meant to be kind so I bit back my sharp reply.

"What you need," she said, "is some hot chicken soup."

The last thing I wanted right now was to have Mrs. Wachtel hovering over me and forcing hot chicken soup down my throat.

"I appreciate it, I really do, Angela and thank your

mom for me, but I'm really better off staying at home."

It took me a while to get rid of her, but I had made up my mind.

Unthinkingly, I slipped out of my clothes and into a nightgown. I heard an odd clunk when I threw my jeans over the back of a chair, and I realized I still had Harry's key. Suddenly I wasn't sure that I'd simply forgotten to give it back. Somewhere in the back of my mind I knew I might want to use it sometime.

Sighing, I slipped into bed with a book and sat up reading until after midnight. The pain was like a tight band around my chest. Now I could never tell Quentin I was sorry. I could never explain that I still loved him. I have no idea what time it was when I finally fell asleep.

The digital light on the microwave glowed in the dark. 3:17. The refrigerator motor hummed and pale slivers of the streetlight came in the kitchen window and made a herringbone pattern on my nightgown. My toes were cold and my finger hurt. Confused, I realized I was standing in the kitchen. I held my hand up to my face, peering closely at it in the uneven light, and a drop of blood fell to the kitchen floor. Quickly and instinctively I reached for a paper towel and pressed it to the cut finger. My heart thumped painfully hard, and my breath was ragged. What had brought me from my bed to the kitchen? And how had I gotten here without realizing it? Even more strange the kitchen looked as if it had been ransacked. All the cabinet doors were open. Every kitchen drawer had been pulled out. The oven door was open and the faint oven light cast a soft illumination over the strange scene. Clutching the paper towel to my bleeding finger, I ran to the kitchen door and tried it. It was dead-bolted tightly. I rushed then to the front door. Locked. The tiles of the floor were icy under my bare feet and a shiver wracked me. Glancing to the right, I was startled to see that the drawers to the little desk in the living room had been pulled out. Even the record cabinet door was open. Yet the television set and the stereo sat undisturbed. If burglars had come they had gotten in without leaving a mark and had taken nothing.

I went back to my bedroom and groped in my closet for my bathrobe. My closet door was open and all my dresser drawers had been pulled out. Even the suitcase under my bed had been pulled out and opened.

I bent to close the suitcase. As I pushed it under the bed, I had the odd sensation that my fingers remembered touching its dimpled surface. I knew then what must have happened. I knew then that I was the one who had opened the drawers and the cabinets. I was the intruder in my own house.

I went back to the kitchen and began methodically closing drawers and cabinets. The knife that had cut me lay on the kitchen table, pink with blood along the blade. I had been sleepwalking—that much was clear. Somehow I had ended up in the kitchen yet before I woke up I had opened every drawer and cabinet in the house. For some reason I had picked up the knife by the blade and had accidentally cut myself. But why? To move it? To defend myself? I wiped the knife blade off on a paper towel and put it back in the drawer where it belonged.

Obviously, I had been looking for something . . . someone. Then the truth hit me with a force like deep pain. I realized, with a terrible contraction of my heart, that I had been looking for Quentin.

Chapter 10

First thing in the morning I went to the gray police station uptown to give them my statement. The police officer was a kindly, balding man. On his index finger he wore a rubber thimble for turning pages. A large white-faced clock hung on the wall behind the counter looking ponderous, as if time were extra heavy at police headquarters.

I told him my story as calmly as I could manage.

"You recognized him right away?" he asked.

I hesitated. "Not when I saw just his hand and his arm." I gulped. "I guess I panicked then and sort of thrashed forward and the tiger backed off. Then I saw his face." I closed my eyes.

"That's when you recognized him?"

"Yes."

Somehow I had expected him to ask me more questions than he did. I wasn't quite sure why, but when we had finished and he told me I could go, I felt vaguely dissatisfied.

He smiled. "You can go now," he repeated.

Reluctantly, I stood up.

I drove from the police station to school feeling as if I'd had a dose of anesthetic. I knew I couldn't even allow myself to think about Quentin.

When I signed in at the office the secretary looked

at me curiously. "Reason for tardiness—required to make statement at police station." I got to the main classroom building just as people were changing classes for third period. In the hall a couple of people I didn't even know were crying. "Blythe!" Biff cried. He clutched me to him tightly. "God, it's awful," he said gruffly. "I just can't believe it."

"I can't let myself think about it," I said. "If I do I'll fall apart."

"He wouldn't want us to cry," Biff choked out. "I know he wouldn't. Jeez, this is so grim. I keep thinking any minute he's going to walk in and it's all going to turn out to be a joke or something. I feel stupid, going on with school like this like nothing happened. Do you know what I mean?" His brown eyes pleaded with me.

"Yeah," I said heavily. "I know."

He gave my shoulder a squeeze and then fled.

I saw Matt Milner dip hurriedly into his class, avoiding me. Did he blame me for Quentin's death? I wondered. Did he think it was somehow my fault because I had broken up with him? I suppose it was just that he couldn't figure out whether to treat me as chief mourner or not, so he had just sheared off when he saw me. That made me appreciate Biff's warmth toward me even more.

I looked around for Elizabeth. She was bound to know more about what the police had found out than I did. At last, I tracked her down and cornered her by the water fountain on the ground floor of A wing. "Tell me what you know, Elizabeth," I insisted. "Everything you've been able to find out about Quentin. What did the police tell his parents?" My hands were gripping the strap of my book bag so tightly that my palms hurt.

"He was dead before the tigers got to him," she said. "If that's what you're worrying about. There would have been a lot more blood, you see—" Her voice trailed off. "Quentin's dad kept screaming that they ought to shoot the tigers, but the police said the tigers didn't have anything to do with it. They found Quentin's car on a side road that runs behind the Croger place and a piece of his shirt was still caught on the top of the fence there, so it looks like he must have tried to climb the fence and lost his balance and fell. His skull was fractured." She grimaced. "The tigers must have found his body and dragged it over into the bushes." She dabbed at her eyes. "I don't know what he was doing out there. He told his parents he was going to see somebody and he just never came back."

"At least," I said bitterly, "the police won't be getting 'weird' about the tigers. Harry will be so relieved."

"What?" Elizabeth looked at me blankly.

"Nothing. Go ahead."

"Are you sure you should have come to school today?" She eyed me uneasily, as if she expected me to burst into flame any minute.

"I'm okay," I said. "I've already been to the police and given them my statement. If I can do that, I can certainly handle school."

"When you found him"—she hesitated—"was he very—messed up? Had the tigers—done anything to him? I heard they eat the soft parts first."

My stomach clutched. "I don't know, Elizabeth. After I realized it was Quentin, my brain just sort of shut down. I wasn't taking it all in."

"It must have been awful." She regarded me with fascinated horror. "Seeing him like that."

"I keep telling myself that it couldn't have happened, that it's all a mistake."

"I think he must have been trying to play a joke on Harry. You know how Quentin was—always wanting to have a good time." Elizabeth dabbed at her eyes.

"Did he—did he say anything to anybody about playing a joke?"

"No, but then he wouldn't, would he? Not to his parents, anyway."

"It doesn't make sense!" I cried. I was sure that if Quentin had wanted to play a joke on Harry, he would have done it at school where it would have embarrassed Harry most. It was like that old puzzle—does a tree make a noise if it falls in the forest and no one hears? A practical joke played at the Croger mansion would have been invisible and therefore nonsensical.

"Quentin's parents thought he seemed kind of upset before he went out," Elizabeth said. "But that doesn't tell us anything. Everybody knows he's been upset ever since you two broke up."

I felt a stabbing pain in my chest. The lockers swam in my vision and I had to steady myself against the wall. Elizabeth was watching me with ghoulish curiosity, waiting to see if I was going to faint. I was glad to disappoint her.

I took a deep breath. "I think Quentin would have gotten somebody to go along with him if he were going to play a joke on Harry," I insisted, taking a deep breath.

"Well, if anybody else was in on it, they're not admitting it. Not that it matters, now. Poor Quentin."

Elizabeth's explanation seemed all wrong to me. I simply wasn't convinced it had happened the way the police said. One thing remained like rock beneath the crashing waves of emotion that shook me—Quentin's death didn't add up and nothing could make me believe that it did.

"He didn't suffer," Elizabeth went on. "He died pretty much instantly."

I remembered how much I had always disliked Elizabeth. Why was I talking to her? To get information, I reminded myself. I needed information. I could have used a shoulder to cry on, as a matter of fact, but that was out of the question. For years it had been Quentin's shoulder I used.

I backed off, anxious to put distance between me and Elizabeth's ghoulishly earnest face. "Thanks for filling me in," I said.

"I knew you'd want to know what happened," she said. "And you couldn't very well ask his parents, could you?"

Even later, in class, I could hear her voice ringing in my ears. "He didn't suffer. I knew you'd want to know what happened." Time seemed to drag incredibly. Minutes were like hours and memories of Quentin filled my brain to bursting.

When I met Harry at lunch, he was quiet. I had to keep my eyes on him to assure myself that he really was sitting across from me. He was unusually subdued even for him and was eating the school meat loaf without comment.

"Snowball and Pixie would never hurt anybody," he began defensively.

I looked at him in amazement. "Nobody thinks the tigers killed him, Harry. Is that what's bothering you? Nobody even cares about the tigers."

Harry prodded his meat loaf with his fork. "I just hope some yahoo doesn't come out to the house and go after Snowball and Pixie with a high-powered rifle. I told Dad we'd better keep them penned up in back until this thing dies down."

I reminded myself that Harry had known the tigers since he was a little kid and that he scarcely knew Quentin at all. That thought was the only thing that kept me from reaching across the table and shaking him.

"Harry, I don't think I'm going to be able to come over to your house anymore. I mean, after what's happened just the thought of it—I can't face it."

"That's okay," he said. "I understand."

"I expect you can get somebody else to tutor you."

"It's okay. After what happened, we might be moving away from here anyway."

"Naturally, you want to find a nice safe place for the tigers," I said.

"Yeah. That's right." He had noticed no hint of irony in my voice. "With this story being in the papers and everything, people might start poking around the place and try to hurt Snowball and Pixie. Dad and Karl like to keep a low profile and this pretty much shoots that, if you know what I mean."

"I went to the police station this morning and made my statement," I said abruptly.

"Yeah, I did that, too, last night."

"They didn't ask me many questions."

"What kind of questions could they ask?" Harry looked at me. "What are you getting at, Blythe?"

"It wasn't a natural death. I thought that meant they had to do a thorough investigation."

"Heck, it was an accident pure and simple!" he exclaimed.

"I guess."

"What do you mean you 'guess.' That's what the police said. For some unknown, incredibly stupid reason Quentin tried to climb the fence and fell and fractured his skull. Case closed. You aren't going to try to make trouble, are you? Because the last thing we need is the police nosing around the house with Dad and Karl behind schedule on their work as it is."

"I'd certainly hate for your dad's work schedule to be disarranged just because Quentin got killed," I said icily.

"It was an accident."

"Maybe. But it doesn't add up."

"What are you trying to say?"

"I don't know. But I have some questions and I'm going to try to get some answers."

"It was an accident. Don't make things worse than they are. Let it be, Blythe."

"Don't try to tell me what to do." There was a long silence as we regarded each other angrily. I knew he was worried about the tigers and I did my best to sympathize, but it was hard.

"The funeral's on Saturday. Are you planning to go?" I asked at last.

He recoiled. "God, no. I hardly knew the guy, Blythe. What would I be doing at the funeral? Besides, we're going to be out of town. Dad wants to check out a magic act that's playing in Raleigh this weekend, and we're all going. Why? Do you need a ride?"

"No. I'll be fine by myself."

"If you want me to take you, just say so."

"No, I'll be okay."

"All right, then."

It seemed as if I was getting on bad terms with everybody. I was touchy with Elizabeth and then I was bristly with Harry. You might have thought I was trying to prove to myself that I didn't have a friend in the world.

When I got home after school, a letter from Dad was waiting in the mailbox. I ripped it open.

Dear Puddleduck,

They've gone and done it. We're over in some place that I can't name but I think they'll allow me to say it's the most Godforsaken stretch of land I've ever seen in my life. I am enclosing a sample of the sand. Everywhere I look I see khaki—not my favorite color. I have made friends with a guy who is a florist who hates it as much as I do. He says his business is going to hell with him away. At least I don't have that to worry about.

My job here is to count jeeps and guns and legal pads when they arrive and to check them off a list. Then they disappear. Heaven only knows what happens to them after that.

You can write me at the APO number on the envelope.

Love,
Dad

I glanced up at the darkening sky. Clouds were gathering overhead and the air was damp. A fitful breeze rustled the leaves. I took the letter inside and re-read it several times. Dad's world seemed so much more normal and safe than mine did—just the reverse of what I had expected. I had been worried that Dad would die, and Quentin had died instead. How weird life was!

I could scarcely remember anymore how much

Dad had annoyed me. I even missed his silliness. Perhaps I would fly to Oregon to stay with Grandmother. There was nothing to stop me from driving to the Raleigh-Durham airport and booking a ticket to Oregon on Dad's charge card. Grandma would be surprised to see me, of course, but she would be pleased. Now that Quentin was dead and things were so tense between Harry and me, staying home didn't seem like such a great idea. I laid Dad's letter down on the kitchen table.

Just the thought of going to Grandma's, crazy as it seemed, cheered me up. It was possible to run away from my troubles, I thought. But not until after the funeral. My eyes suddenly blurred with tears.

I put a TV dinner in the microwave for supper. It was a long time since I had remembered to eat and I devoured the food hungrily. After supper I finished my homework, more out of habit than anything else. I tried to watch a sitcom on television but the laugh tracks—mechanical, inhuman bursts of laughter that didn't seem to be attached to anything, gave me the creeps. Finally I switched off the set.

When it got dark, I did a double check of the locks on the doors and windows, but even after I had reassured myself they were securely locked I was stiff with fear. Locks could keep burglars out, but they couldn't keep me in. From the kitchen I could hear the faint whiz of the traffic outside, heading out to the bypass. If I had been foolish enough to pick up a knife blade in my sleep, what was to stop me from walking out on the highway and standing there, my nightgown flapping around my ankles? The trucks barreling off the bypass would never stop in time.

Sometime later I managed to go to sleep. I'm not sure how long it was before I woke and sat up suddenly in my bed. My first overwhelming feeling when I became conscious of the texture of the bedspread under my fingertips was relief. I was in bed, after all. I was where I was supposed to be. I hadn't been sleepwalking. Then I became aware of a creeping sense of unease. Rain drummed steadily on the roof. I wished it would stop so I could hear better. Fear hovered on the edge of my consciousness. But all the sounds I could hear now were soft and familiar. Outside, a truck whizzed by with a rising and falling sound. I sat rigid in the bed for a moment, holding my breath, listening so hard I hurt with the effort. Then I slipped out of bed and reached for my robe. As an afterthought, I picked the glass paperweight up off my desk and gripped it tightly in my palm. Holding my breath, I glided quietly out of the bedroom. I glanced into Dad's bedroom, then moved down the hall. Standing at the open door to the kitchen, I listened to the rain spray against the kitchen windows with a whispering whoosh. I could barely make out the comforting rumble of the refrigerator. I realized then that with the rain there was too much background noise for me to have heard any intruder unless he had broken glass. It would have had to be some sharp sound. Breathing quickly now, I switched on the lights. No one in the kitchen. I went to the back door and tested the knob. Locked fast. While I was standing at the back door, I switched on the floodlight. Its beam shot through a shower of crystal drops reaching only as far as the car before it was lost to darkness. No one was out there, I told myself. I was alone in the house. Then I whirled around suddenly, my heart in my throat. But nothing was behind me. Dad's letter fluttered on the kitchen table, disturbed by my sudden movement. I ran to the front door. But it, too, was locked. In the living room rain beat on the windows in a monotonously even rhythm, the sound muffled by the draperies that hung heavy and still against the big window.

Shivering uncontrollably now, I returned to my bedroom and slipped under the covers. My ears strained, but I still heard only the steady rain and the faint whizzing of trucks. Yet something must have wakened me. Thunder? Rain whispered overhead, the steady even sound of a downpour that had settled into a regular rhythm. It seemed as if I sat in the bed listening in the darkness for hours, but I suppose I must have finally fallen asleep.

When I woke, a faint morning light leaked around my curtains. I was stiff and tired, but deeply thankful it was morning. Daytime was safe. People in the neighborhood would be up and about soon. It was Saturday, the day of Quentin's funeral.

I leapt out of bed and pulled on a pair of wool slacks and a turtleneck. Water dripped from the eaves, falling with irregular plops into the puddles. When I stepped out the door a cold drop hit the top of my head. I moved quickly out from under the dripping. Mrs. Holloman, our neighbor, was in her driveway picking up her morning paper.

My nerves might be shredded beyond repair, but unbelievably, in the neighborhood, life went on as usual. I saw the Mercers' station wagon, stuffed to the gills with camping equipment, drive off pulling a boat. The old man a few blocks down was taking his Pomeranian for a walk. I brought the morning paper inside, but I didn't open it. I was afraid it might have a picture of Quentin and I was struggling hard to keep my composure as it was. I kept glancing out the window though I knew it made no sense. I was acting as if I were afraid someone would sneak up on me and that was ridiculous. Quentin's death had unnerved me.

At two, I went to the Episcopal church downtown. A book stood on a pedestal near the door for people to sign, and I added my name to the rest before going in. Inside, the altar was heaped with flowers and the sharp outlines of the coffin at the front were partly hidden by the blanket of greenery and flowers. It was hard to believe Quentin's body was inside that coffin. The chrysanthemums draped over the polished wood looked artificial and the entire scene, from the stained glass windows to the tall brass candlesticks, seemed like a stage set. Or was it just me? I felt like a puppet, as if some unseen malignant force had arranged this terrible scene and forced me to be a player in it. Around me people shuffled their feet and spoke in inaudible murmurs, looking thoroughly uncomfortable.

In the front pew, a nurse dressed in white sat next to Quentin's mother, holding her hand. I don't think Mrs. Bonner even realized what was going on. Her doctor must have overdone it on the tranquilizers. The back of Mr. Bonner's neck was freckled and his head jerked as if he were palsied. Quentin's dad had gotten old overnight. I heard a muffled sob behind me.

I couldn't help thinking that Quentin would have enjoyed himself if he could have been there. He would have loved the flowers and formality. Most of all he would have loved being the center of attention.

Already my handkerchief was a sodden mess that was no good to me, and my nose was so stopped up I was gasping for breath. The organ music ebbed and the service began but I was scarcely conscious of what the priest was saying.

What could have made Quentin go over to Harry's house to climb that fence all alone at night? I wondered. Quentin had been suspicious of Harry, I remembered, and had wondered about the purpose of the fence around the property. Could he have been doing a little investigating? Did he think somehow he was going to get something on Harry or his dad? Certainly that made more sense than Elizabeth's practical joke theory. But I couldn't get past my feeling that something was wrong with both ideas. Quentin would have taken one of his friends with him. He had never been a loner. Even if he was studying, he always wanted an audience nearby.

The drone of the minister's voice had stopped and the congregation stood for a hymn. I groped in the hymnal frantically, trying to find the place. At last the book fell open to page 449. "My Faith Looks Up To Thee." I stared at the line in a trance of thought, while stout voices sang around me. "Fear and distrust remove; O bear me safe above . . ." It was all I could do to keep from crying out. Suddenly I knew that Quentin had never fallen from that fence to his death. He never would have climbed the fence in the first place. He was afraid of heights.

I knew now that his death was no accident.

Chapter 11

As soon as the last strains of the organ died away, I made a break for my car. I was one of the first ones out of the parking lot. When I caught a glimpse of my face in the rearview mirror I was shocked to see that it was wet with tears. I had been thinking so hard I was scarcely aware of the tears streaming down my face. Groping in my purse for a tissue, I hastily wiped my eyes.

A kaleidoscope of images tumbled in my mind—the motorcyclist a dark presence in my rearview mirror, Harry's untidy ash-blond hair, the rabbit hiding in Harry's hat, the shaggy head of the tiger, and for some reason the girl on the stretcher the night of the crash, her face ominously white. I wasn't sure how everything fit together yet, but I had a feeling I knew where I could find the answers.

I went back home and into my bedroom. In my jewelry box was the key with the tiger charm. Maybe I had been suspicious of Harry even the day we had found Quentin's body. Why else had I kept the key? I dug a pair of binoculars out of Dad's dresser, left over from his birdwatching days. It would be smart to check out the place at a distance before I tried to get in.

My heart pounding, I got in my car. Maybe I was

making a terrible mistake, but I knew I had to take the chance.

In a matter of minutes I had pulled up in front of the tall gates of the Croger mansion. In a few places I could make out the upper floors of the mansion through the trees. I got a closer look with the binoculars. No signs of activity that I could see, but I needed to be sure. Something was odd. I squinted at the house a moment, then put the binoculars up to my eyes and took a second look. One of the windows on the second story looked different—the glass was clearer, newer looking than the other glass. It didn't have that faint violet look that old glass gets in the sunlight.

I rang the bell. It seemed as if I stood there forever but there was no crackle of static. No one had turned on the radio receiver inside. They really were all gone. I glanced at my car, wondering if I should take this risk. If what I thought was true, Harry was a murderer. Maybe I should simply go to the police. But with what? I didn't have a particle of evidence.

I put the key in the gate and turned it. The lock swung open smoothly. My heart leapt inside me like a fish. It was going to work—I was getting in.

My body had recoiled as I drove toward the house, as if it had its own memory of the Croger mansion and shrank from it. Yet at the same time I wondered if I were imagining things. It seemed incredible that Harry could have murdered Quentin. What possible motive could he have?

The garage door did not lift open automatically and I was not sure how to get it open, so I parked in front of the house. I was relieved to see no sign of tigers. I unlocked the front door and pulled it closed behind me.

My heart seemed stuck somewhere in my throat as I made my way up the shadowy stairs. Light leaked through the colored glass and stained my fingers blue as I reached the second floor and my hand shook. I wasn't sure which room had the apparently new window, but I had a strong hunch. With each step I made on the Oriental rug, the wood creaked faintly under my weight and I had to force myself to breathe normally.

I opened the door to the study and stepped in. Its marble floor, the tiles arranged in black and white squares like a checkerboard, reminded me that I was playing a game. A dangerous game.

The room was just the same, I thought at first. No. I stopped suddenly in my tracks. The room was not the same. The window panes in the window *had* been replaced. I went over to the window and touched the new putty along the edges of the glass. It was a sloppy job. Harry had probably replaced the panes himself. I wondered what his father thought about the broken window.

A glimmer in my peripheral vision made me look down suddenly. Something shiny was on the floor behind the radiator. I gasped when I recognized, half-hidden under the radiator, the Tiffany knife I had given Quentin for Christmas. It was open, its blade broken off, and his initials, Q.E.B., were clearly visible in ornate script on the sheath of the knife.

Just then I heard the door to the room open and I turned around suddenly. Harry stood in the open doorway, smiling. "Blythe," he said. "What brings you here to visit us? Not that I'm not always glad to see you."

"I—I came to return your key. I accidentally walked off with it and I came to bring it back."

He laughed. "Keep going. I'm enjoying this. And what brought you up to the study? Maybe you left an algebra book up here or something?" His gaze had wandered to the algebra book lying on the desk. "Come on, I'm sure you can think of some reason or other for coming up here. Just keep working on it."

"You killed Quentin, didn't you?" I blurted out.

He closed the door behind him and walked over to me. When he touched me I cringed but he only patted his hands briskly over my body.

"Just checking to make sure you aren't wired for sound." He laughed. "We came back early, as you see. The performance was cancelled. The magician had the flu. But that's okay. I wouldn't have missed this little meeting of ours for the world. Here we are together, all alone."

I didn't care for his expression. "I left word where I was just in case I shouldn't come back," I said, wishing now that I had. My furious anger at Harry had subsided now and I was beginning to be afraid.

Harry leisurely fished a bronze letter opener out of his back pocket. He must have carefully removed it before trapping Quentin in the room, I realized. Now he had brought it back to replace it right before my eyes, just as though nothing had happened. The audacity of the gesture took my breath away.

"*Why?* What I don't understand is why you did it?" I cried.

"I didn't mean to kill him so fast." He looked a little embarrassed. "I wanted to make him wait a lot longer, but I heard this noise and ran in and it turned out Quentin had kicked through the window. I guess I panicked because there was no way he could get out what with the bars and all. I guess I just didn't think.

I grabbed one of those weighted bookends over there and whopped him over the head." Harry shook his head. "Didn't know my own strength as it turned out."

"Are you out of your mind?" I cried.

"He got what was coming to him." Harry's voice hardened. "I wish I'd made him suffer more. I wanted to make him suffer the way Caroline did."

"Caroline?" I was having trouble taking in what he said.

"My sister," said Harry patiently. "Remember the wreck Quentin was in when he was drunk?"

The blond girl who was in the wreck. She was Harry's sister? "But her name wasn't Weaver," I said, confused. "I read the newspaper story about the wreck. I would have noticed if you and she had the same name. Hers was something unusual."

"Weaver is Dad's stage name," said Harry impatiently. "I use it now that I've moved in with him, but our legal name's Rassmussen."

"Harry R. Weaver," he had told me that night at the dance, "and I won't tell you what the R. is for."

"Quentin killed her," Harry went on. "He killed her just the same as if he'd held a gun to her head. Then he went on with his life like nothing happened. God, it grated on me to see him laughing and making jokes around school."

"Harry, he was sorry about it. He really was."

"Sorry?" Harry yelled. "He didn't know what sorry was. And the law couldn't touch him. He murdered her and he got away with it! Well, now I've fixed him."

"Two wrongs don't make a right," I said weakly.

Harry laughed. "Pretty sanctimonious, aren't we?

You helped me, you know. Quentin wouldn't have given me the time of day if I hadn't had you. He hated it when you dumped him and did I love watching him squirm!"

I knew then why Harry had said, that night at the dance, "You're the only one that will do." I was the bait to lure Quentin to his death.

"I told him I had to talk to him about you." Harry tested the sharpness of the letter opener against his forefinger. "I told him not to mention it to anybody, but that we had to talk and it was urgent. He came right on out, pretty as you please, and I ushered him up here to this room." Harry's face darkened. "It was stupid of him to try to get out the window. He could never get out and he only messed up his arms trying."

"That's why you needed the tigers, isn't it?" I said, the truth dawning. "You had to cover up the cuts on his arms."

"I didn't like it, but I didn't have any choice. I had to tell Dad. I couldn't do it by myself. He was pretty shook, but I knew that he wouldn't let me be sent up for murder—he'd already lost Caroline. Karl was away, so that was no problem. We got the body outside and let Snowball and Pixie out. After they'd chewed over him all night there was no way to tell he had cut himself."

My stomach heaved.

"What I can't figure out is how did you guess?" he asked softly.

"Quentin was afraid of heights. I knew he wouldn't have tried to climb that fence."

Harry smiled. "He must have climbed the fence, though, huh? I mean, you don't have a bit of proof that he didn't. We never had this little talk and you don't have any proof."

"You're right," I said. "I don't have any proof." My mind was racing. Quentin's knife was under the radiator. That was evidence. And as far as a motive, once I told the police where to look, they would be able to make the connection between Caroline's death and Quentin's. Even if Caroline had used a different last name, it would be easy enough for the police to find out that Harry was her brother. What I had to concentrate on was convincing Harry that I wasn't going to go to the cops.

"I knew the wreck was his fault," I said. "I couldn't stand knowing what he'd done to that girl. Why do you think I broke up with him?"

"And here I thought it was that you couldn't resist me." He eyed me curiously. "Go on. Keep talking. I'm interested."

"I don't approve of your taking the law into your own hands. But I do understand why you did it. I won't tell anybody."

Harry laughed softly. "You are incredible, Blythe. So cool! I never could tell what you were thinking."

"Well, now I'm telling you."

"Right. And that's great. I love it. But maybe you've already told somebody what you're thinking?" He raised an eyebrow. "You were suspicious of me as soon as we found the body, right?"

"No! I haven't talked to anybody about it. Besides, I've decided to go live with my grandmother and put all this behind me."

Harry opened the desk drawer, slid the letter opener in, and closed the drawer. "Oh?" he said casually. "Where does she live?"

"Washington, D.C.," I lied. "I feel it's time for me to start fresh."

"Funny thing." His shoulders moved and when he turned around I saw that he was laughing silently. "That's kind of what Dad and I have in mind, too."

"I guess this is so long, then."

"I guess it is." He was smiling as he picked up the heavy bookend and turned toward me.

The muscles at the back of my neck tensed. Suddenly, I grabbed the algebra book and pitched it at him. I scarcely even registered the look of astonishment on his face as the book hit him. I darted past him to the door, flung it open, and dashed for the stairs. Stumbling, I half-fell down the stairs. I could hear his steps thundering in the hall behind me.

"Dad!" His voice echoed in the hallway. "It's Blythe! She knows! She's getting away!"

I heard a door slam upstairs and footsteps thundering down the stairs as I reached the front door. I slammed the door shut behind me with some vague idea of delaying them. Already my car keys were in my hand. Luckily I hadn't locked the door. I ran down the front steps and jumped into my car. When I turned on the ignition, to my relief, the engine leapt to life. I felt as if I were moving in slow motion but the speedometer veered steadily upward as I stepped on the gas. A moment later the closed gates loomed ahead of me. The key that would open them was still in my pocket, but I was afraid to stop. I slowed the car thinking that perhaps I should ram the gates, but they looked so strong that at the last minute, my nerve gave way. I left the engine running as I jumped out of the car. I unlocked the gate and kicked it open. My hands were trembling when I got back in the car.

I thought I could hear the whining sound of the mansion's garage door opening. With only a quick look over my shoulder, I stepped on the accelerator and sped out the gate.

Chapter 12

The bypass was the fastest route to the airport, but getting to it would take me directly past the Croger mansion and Harry or his dad could be watching. I couldn't risk it. The road that ran by the parapsychology lab would get me to the Raleigh-Durham airport as surely as the bypass road and I figured making it to the airport was my only hope to get away. No matter where I went in town, they could catch up with me. The two of them could separate, and for all I knew one might be lying in wait right now by the police station, ready to cut me off if I went that way. No place around here was safe for me now. They knew my car. Harry knew who my friends were. Where could I hide?

Ahead I saw the familiar Holmhaven subdivision sign with its bed of struggling chrysanthemums. It looked so safe, but I knew I didn't dare turn in there. That would be the first place they would look for me. I kept going on the main road instead.

I checked my rearview mirror but to my surprise no one was behind me. Had I really lost them? Relief washed over me so strongly I felt weak with it.

I realized now that it must have been Harry on his dad's motorcycle who had followed me and trashed my car that night weeks ago. His calmly trashing my car for brushing past him was like a preview to his cold-blooded plot to kill Quentin. Clearly his sister's death had left Harry completely unhinged, and his father would go along with anything to protect his only surviving child. Now I knew too much about what had happened at the mansion. Harry and his father wouldn't hesitate to kill me too.

The winter sun was a low pale blur in the sky and the shadows were long as I drove past the row of cheap houses on Hammond Road. Piece of cake, I thought, feeling the muscles in the back of my neck loosen. I was almost out of this town. Then I saw the car in my rearview mirror. It was far back, but it looked to me like a light-colored sedan. It wasn't Harry's car; I could tell that much. But could I be sure it wasn't his father's? I recalled the white Volvo I'd seen in the garage the first day I'd gone to the mansion. There was one way to find out. When I reached the edge of downtown, almost deserted now on a Saturday, I ran through the first three red lights. The white car behind me didn't stop either.

Then I knew. My stomach squeezed in panic. I stepped on the gas suddenly and heard a protesting cough from the old engine. I wished I were driving a new car, but at least mine did have a big V-8 engine. I sent the speedometer up to eighty, ignoring the car's ominous shuddering.

If I had any lingering hope that the white car was innocent, it vanished when I hit a hundred and the Volvo behind me kept pace. My whole body prickled with fear as I glanced over my shoulder. They were closer now, gaining on me. Probably they were going to ram me.

I could make out two people in the car. Soon they

were close enough that I could make out their faces in my rearview mirror. Harry and his dad.

I glanced at the speedometer, the needle now quivering at over a hundred. I had never gone so fast and I was surprised at how normal it felt, except for the vibration of the car. Then I heard an ominous knocking. The car couldn't give out on me now! I held fiercely onto the wheel, afraid of losing control. Suddenly I felt a jolt. The Volvo had bumped me. Glancing over my shoulder, I saw Mr. Weaver grimace as he wrenched his steering wheel to the left. The white car pulled out beside me. They were going to try to run me off the road!

We were coming fast upon the curve that went past the quarry. With a sinking of the heart I remembered that Harry and his father knew this road well. They could run me off the road right at the quarry.

I pressed against the accelerator and pulled ahead of them. I prayed my car would hold to the ground around the curve. It slid heartstoppingly into a skid. But miraculously the car regained its traction. The guardrail flashed by me on my right. A loud pop issued from the engine and smoke wisped from the hood. In desperation, I floored the accelerator.

I knew my car was spurting oil. The road behind me was covered with it. Soon my engine would freeze and though the Volvo had dropped back, Harry and his dad were still close on my tail. Coming off the curve, my car was losing power. Glancing behind me, I instinctively cringed against the expected impact. But no! The Volvo skated crazily across the road and crashed into the metal rail. I turned around and saw a ragged-edged gap in the railing.

My car coasted powerlessly to a halt. I sat shivering for some minutes. I wondered what I would do if they got out of their wrecked car and came after me. The silence was eerie.

I knew I wasn't far from the parapsychology lab. On Saturday it would be locked, but it should be easy for me to break a window, get in, and use the phone.

At last, gathering my courage, I unlocked my door and walked tentatively over to the gap in the railing. I was shaky enough at the knees that my steps were halting. The narrow limestone and sand shoulder of the road fell away rapidly to the water-filled quarry below. A jay flew over my head, warning me with a hoarse cry. I had expected to see the wrecked car below, but I saw only the roughly lapping waves of the water in the quarry. The water was churning from the car that had sunk so quickly beneath its surface. A spreading pool of oil on the water reflected rainbow colors. I hugged myself, suddenly cold.

I didn't hear the car drive up. I only became conscious of the sound of its motor when a familiar voice called my name. "Blythe! What the hell's going on?"

Looking over beyond the guardrail, I saw Biff getting out of his car and I smiled at him. He trotted over to me. "Didn't you see me?" he demanded. "I was coming from Quentin's house after the funeral wondering where you were when all of a sudden I saw you streaking by on Hammond Road going at the speed of light and half a second later this other car came right after you. What was going on? And why's your car just sitting there in the middle of the road?" He glanced at the slick of oil on the road. "Is the car dead? Do you need a ride back? What got into you, driving that fast? You scared me to death. I thought I was going to be pulling you out of a wreck when I caught up."

I leaned my head on his chest and burst into tears.

Chapter 13

That evening, I sat in front of Angela's fireplace wrapped in an old afghan and sipping Angela's mom's homemade chicken soup out of a blue and white mug.

Biff was on a hassock at my feet. The Wachtel family buzzed around the great room popping corn, pouring out soft drinks, and murmuring their concern.

"I won't hear of you going back to your house," Mrs. Wachtel said, placing a large bowl of popcorn in front of Biff. "What an idea! It's ridiculous for you to live in that house alone. We have plenty of room now that Jim's away at college and besides it won't be for long. Your father will be home before you know it. You just move your things into our extra room until your dad gets back."

The phone rang. Angela's dad went in the kitchen to answer it.

"You better take her up on the offer, Blythe," suggested Biff. "Remember, your car's pretty much done for. You're going to need to share transportation anyway."

"I'll take you up on that offer," I told Mrs. Wachtel promptly.

Mr. Wachtel returned from the kitchen looking grim. "They just brought up the car on a dredging hook. The boy and his father were still in it. Dead, of course."

I shuddered, remembering how much I had liked Harry before I discovered the truth.

Mr. Wachtel frowned. "The police couldn't tell me much. When they went out to the Croger mansion, the gate was open and this fellow Karl was just driving in. He seemed to be completely confused and said he didn't know anything about what had happened. I guess he's probably telling the truth."

"Just the same, I'd better stick close by you for a few days," said Biff. "Keep an eye on you."

I was sure I had nothing to worry about now that Harry and his dad were dead, but I smiled at Biff gratefully. "I never thought I'd be glad I was driving such an old car, but you know if Dad's old heap hadn't sprung that major oil leak, I'd be history now."

"Hey, I wasn't that far behind you," Biff pointed out.

"Next time, Blythe, honey, go to the police when you find a murderer," said Mrs. Wachtel earnestly. "You had a real close call. Just thinking about it scares me to death."

"I didn't really have any evidence until I actually got in the study and found Quentin's knife there," I pointed out. "I knew something was wrong—I knew Quentin hadn't climbed that fence because he was terrified of heights, but that was no proof. I might have been just making it up."

"I didn't know he was afraid of heights," confessed Biff. "It's only when you mention it that I realize he, like, never went up on the monkey bars when we were kids." He wiped his eyes.

"So you see, all I had to go on was my own hunch and that didn't amount to much."

"You took a big risk," said Angela.

"I guess when I realized how Harry had used me, I was too mad to care."

"You're too brave for your own good, young lady," said Mr. Wachtel sternly.

"She took care of the creep that murdered Quentin, didn't she?" Biff punched his fist into his hand. "It all worked out. I'm not losing any sleep over those two, I'm telling you."

"I can't believe Harry killed Quentin," said Angela dolefully. "I can understand his feelings about his poor sister. It was awful! But to lure Quentin out there and trap him like an animal—it was so cold-blooded!"

I thought about all the people who had died—Caroline, Quentin, Harry and his dad—and shivered. I knew better than anyone how close I had come to being added to the list.

"I think what we all need now," said Mrs. Wachtel brightly, "is some hot cocoa and toasted marshmallows."

"Mom!" exclaimed Angela. "Food doesn't solve everything."

"What Blythe needs is a big hug," said Biff. He squeezed me tight, afghan and all, and suddenly my toes were toasty warm.

Firelight danced on the dark tiles of the hearth and the air smelled of popcorn and cinnamon sticks. I looked around at all the friendly faces, pink in the firelight, and wondered why I had felt so alone.

JANICE HARRELL is the author of many popular books for both young adult and adult readers. She lives in North Carolina.